~ Dedicated to Scott William F. Cady

the ne plus ultra of this

Acknowledgement

I wish to acknowledge the excellent friendship and advice provided by Craig Cady, Seth Tucker, and Dave Jamison both in enduring my ongoing sense of self and critiquing both it and a never-ending litany of opinion. However, and most importantly here, for responding to these stories and this collection. I cannot begin to thank my parents enough for bringing me into the playdough and giving me all this opportunity and support. I have been variously called hedonist, epicure, madman, and bon vivant and accept the epithets gladly. I hope this collection inspires you to feel similarly.

I also wish to mention some of the inspiration that drove this need to share. They are not presented in any particular order, but have motivated so much in my life (and yes, some are fictional characters, go figure): Don Quixote, The Reverend Charles Lutwidge Dodgson, A.A. Milne, Inspector Clouseau (Peter Sellers), Antal Szerb, Len Rix, Dave Eggers, Han Shan, Omar Khayyam, Rumi, William Shakespeare, William Carlos Williams, Jan Brueghel, John Irving, Mark Leyner, Hunter S. Thompson, Salman Rushdie, Donovan, Scott McLemee, Ken Wilber, Terry Gilliam, Ignatius J. Reilly, and so many, many more.

Hence my… "*pitifullest infinitesimal fraction of a product*".

"If people bring so much courage to this world the world has to kill them to break them, so of course it kills them. The world breaks everyone and afterward many are strong at the broken places. But those that will not break it kills. It kills the very good and the very gentle and the very brave impartially. If you are none of these, you can be sure it will kill you too but there will be no special hurry."

~Ernest Hemmingway

"It is a happy talent, to know how to play."

~Ralph Waldo Emerson

"To live is to play at the meaning of life."

~Earnest Becker

"And maddest of all, to see life as it is, and not as it should be."

~Don Miguel de Cervantes

Foreward by Dr. Seth Tucker

(A Warning)

This text asks us to dive deep, to wrestle with the old gods of sanity and reason and wealth before Trump was even a glimmer in the mad-eye of white rage, to erupt in a rigor mortis of existential poetical climax or encase our feet in cement and let the darkness or the light of the quixotic take us. Or die trying, which is what John Cady asserts. These essays and poems and inquiries and rants and screeds anticipate the moribund gestalt of our recent awakening to 'the enemy among us' here in the US where we see the divisions even when there aren't any, where the stupid few get to dictate our reality and realities, and where our willingness to believe the old lies of capitalism are whispered or shouted at us as we sleep. Inside this cover, find the animated wisdoms that Cervantes would have cheered wildly for from his perch in a turning windmill.

It's the playdough, stupid.

Seth Brady Tucker is executive director of the *Longleaf Writers' Conference* (which you should endow with riches and plan to attend, every year in the second week of May) and he teaches creative writing at the Lighthouse Writers' Workshop and at the Colorado School of Mines near Denver. He is senior prose editor for the Tupelo Quarterly Review, is originally from Wyoming, and once served as an Army Paratrooper with the 82nd Airborne in Iraq. He is a multi-genre writer and his work recently appeared in the Los Angeles Review, Driftwood, Copper Nickel, Birmingham Poetry Review, and others. He thinks John Cady has totally lost it, and cannot think of any better way to rage against that dying of the light.

https://sethbradytucker.ink/index.html

Prologue

I don't know if it's true or not, but my 'thoughts' or 'life' seem pointless if I cannot find one permanent thing. Maybe that "one thing" is the eternal nature of transience? Truth is a loaded word. One of my favorite sentences in existence is the KDworld.net tagline: "*It's like the truth, only real.*"

Does it make any sense to strip my thought of conceit? My soul of guise? Am I just fooling myself anyway by writing... by questing? Am I nothing but a poor, timid attempt at Don Quixote, protected by the faux-shield of a computer? Would I do better to throw down this enabling cyber-armor and take up this discourse in the streets?

Being the Neo-Frivolist that I learned I am in writing, I wish to invite anyone to experience this as portal into a somewhat unrelatable consciousness as it looks out onto many things. This "consciousness" fears it will never be shared, seen, or remotely understood, but cannot bear the thought of not trying. This will not be a 'story' in the way we have come to think of them, but a glance into the -dare I say soul- of an entity that begs to be exposed.

I promise to say something real or die trying! Of all the ridiculous...

Vini, Vidi, Reliquit!

The following verses between the short stories are all by Omar Khayyam:

XXXIII

Were the choice mine to come, should I have come?
Or to become? What might I have become?
What better fortune could I then have chanced on,
Than not to come, become, or even be?

A HEARTRENDING WORK OF STUPEFYING BRILLIANCE

I might want to write a heartrending work of stupefying brilliance, hmmmm, and maybe even unlimited jouissance, but first I'd have to lose some weight. I live in LA. Not Los Angeles, but "Ellay," and in this metropolitan celebration of exoterics it is not so much what you do, but how you look doing it.

I admit this to myself, though it hurts. I plan to use it more as grand stratagem than excuse for procrastination. My writing routine, therefore, includes an exhaustive exercise regimen.

Before I chronicle my literary exploits, I must describe the setting that frames this attempt. I am firmly ensconced in a "*heavenly bed*" – part of a new marketing ploy by the Westin Pasadena in which they make a little cash on the side by branding and selling their painstakingly crafted interior design. My wife (an actress) is lying next to me, trying to read some material that will expand her interests outside of the business. To that end, she is reading a biography about Albert Einstein. She complains that it is frustrating because every time she encounters the word Einstein she thinks "Epstein-Wyckoff &

Associates" – an agency with which she has always aspired to sign. She says she won't be able to make it through page eight if this persists.

My writing regimen shall be threefold at the very least. First, I embark on a high-protein, low-carb diet along the lines of Atkins, but one which I will name after a fictional Swedish scientist. One does not want to hear that one has been laboring under the "second best" diet, or that one's diet methodology has fallen into disfavor. By creating an unassailable fictional diet that is in principle similar to the most popular diet, so much annoyance is avoided. I can even take some joy in imagining curious fellow Angelinos googling "Sverin Renneblad" to no avail. This also allows me to evade all, "*Well my diet...*" conversations, by claiming to be involved with this mystical and secret diet, which prevents me from comparing it to other diets. *"All I can tell you is it's an improvement on Atkins. Can we talk about something else please*?"

Second, I shall have to purchase a number of the magic-diet formulas that are the touchstone of late-night TV. I'm thinking DreamAway™ or Cortislim™ or perhaps even the one that is so good because it's so expensive (it is billed as way too serious for anyone who wants to lose 10-20 "vanity pounds"). It is clearly targeted at the significant cross-demographic of individuals suffering from obesity coupled with the crippling belief that expensive equals effective. This part of my writing regimen (let's call it the 3-magic-diet-program-cocktail) will certainly lead to some loss of weight and perhaps trans-conscious states whereby I can access unknown talents.

Third, I will employ one of the finest Tai-Bo instructors, a life-coach/Scientologist, a personal trainer, and a script doctor. This part of the writing regimen does bring up the specter of plagiarism. I mean how much of my new body will really be my own? However, this is the way things are done in *Ellay* and it is not my position to question. Not if I am to write a heartrending work of stupefying brilliance.

This is where some will suggest a good plastic surgeon and perhaps steroid therapy, but lines have to be drawn somewhere. One cannot simply scratch a few words on paper, let a doctor suck out 50 lbs. of fat, and show up for the Pulitzer nomination announcement. This is writing and good writing is hard work.

Speaking of hard work, it will be difficult for my coaches, late night TV Miracle drugs, workouts, and diet to succeed. I need to lose at least 30 pounds to be considered for a Newberry or Caldecott Medal or even a National Book Award. I would need to lose at least 50 to be in the running for a Pulitzer or Nobel Prize. I've been told that losing 50 pounds in three weeks can be dangerous, but then again, so can literature.

I shall begin writing in earnest on Monday.

XII

A gourd of red wine and a sheaf of Poems
A bare subsistence, half-a-loaf, not more
Supplied us two alone in the free desert:
What Sultan could we envy on his throne?

GAMBLING POETRY

Initially I thought this wanted to take the form of a poem. You know, with inexplicable capitalization, indentation, or punctuation to begin each line. Sometimes employing vaguely random

breaks

and an infatuation with word choice like randomly vague or vaguely random. The difference more important than the seemingly arbitrary interruption on the page—wild gesticulations of arrangement to communicate god knows what. However, this will not take the form of a poem despite being about poetry. It fights for the form of painfully short and probably rambling story, while mocking any attempt to render it otherwise.

It is a metaphor.

It is only a metaphor for writing -my writing- and isn't even as good as Han Shan's infamous suggestion: *"...and on that note you can save your sighs, we could inscribe our poems on biscuits and the homeless dogs wouldn't deign to nibble."* What does it mean when someone's assessment of the nature of your efforts is better than your own?

My metaphor is that of a gambler I chanced to play alongside at a $10 craps table. He was extraordinarily drunk. He bumbled to his proximate position fumbling a bowl of chips sans container with denominations such as $1,000 and $5,000. In his structureless heap, he had more money than my salary would total over two or three years of peak performance. He could not contain the chips; such was their hodgepodge arrangement and his groping instability. He would, at a gesture, send twenty thousand dollars lolling across the floor or bouncing off the table or his neighbor. He had a minder though, a follower, a protector, who would silently swoop in from around and gather this constant splash, tinkle, roll of rainbow-colored representation. While the professionally dressed minder would sprint hither and thither in pursuit of a tumbling pair of purple or burgundy, dodging wayfarers and stretching under accommodations, he seemed to keep a hawkish eye on the inconceivably vertical fountain of cash that was his responsibility. I could not tell if he was employed by the casino or the gentleman, but his urgent presence spoke clearly to the danger of hoping to pick up a stray or two on the sly.

Seeing so much money so ill-kempt and strangely distributed both on and off the table created a great deal of perspective. Not only did it not seem to matter to the possessor where any of it went, it made my 'allowance' of money to gamble this entire weekend seem incomprehensibly meek and somewhat pitiful. I planned to survive an entire weekend with an amount scarcely to be contained in a single chip? Dropping ten times the amount or kicking it across the room would not cause him to bat an eye. He could babble and slur his way through another drink order, though, and no one seemed to mind when he missed the table with a die or two – three or four times in a row. Everyone around politely retrieved his explosions of dice, or chips, or verbal debris, and held their silence while returning their expressions to the wall safe of their awe.

And, somehow, this seems like writing to me, like *my* writing: unkempt piles of thought spun into words and lost on various hard drives, napkins, or notebooks. Drunkenly scattered and whimsically thrust into play, it hasn't any impact. Its histrionic nature, nevertheless, is equally ignored. In fact, one might say it merely aspires to this comparison of insignificance and ignobility. It hasn't even achieved the embarrassing example of its own metaphor, and certainly no one is employing a minder.

LXXIV

Poor ball, struck by Fate's heavy polo mallet,
Running whichever way it drives you, numbed
Of sense, though, He who set you on your course,
He knows, He knows, He knows.

MY ERSTWHILE LIFE

On a Saturday morning after waking slowly, I pick up a book by William Carlos Williams: *Pictures from Brueghel*. I think about the mad painter and the doctor turned poet and wonder how they resonate. This leads me to imagine a world wherein I could set about to make a poem in response to each of Brueghel's paintings. It is such a beautiful world. I long to open the pages of this imagined world and walk in as to a movie or a good book.

Instead on this Saturday, I will continue to look for a job I don't want. Again, I will set my mind on that undesired object of my intention and go about trying to achieve it in the same old distracted way. Perhaps my first effort should be to write down these concerns. Yes, that would be sure to bring me no closer to the abhorred job I abhor not having.

Perhaps, if these concerns are meaningful, I will write something that can change the world over the summer. Well, my world anyway. It's hilarious to express it that way, as it throws into juxtaposition the idea of *writing something in a summer* that would change the world and writing something that would *change the world in a summer*. It's the little bits of life like that -- the little pieces of humor that so tickle my mind that I can see I'm not, and never will be, fit for any kind of sane employment. And it gives me no end of pleasure to imagine how one day I will be free to travel the world and compose poems to the pantheon of Brueghel's work. It somehow reminds me of something I just read. "My life is like trying to drown out the noise of a dying dog in the street...". Yes, I have just read:

To a Dog Injured in the Street

It is myself,
        not the poor beast lying there
                yelping with pain
that brings me to myself with a start-
        as at the explosion
                of a bomb, a bomb that has laid
all the world to waste.
        I can do nothing
                but sing about it
and so I am assuaged
        from my pain.

A drowsy numbness drowns my sense
        as if of hemlock
                I had drunk. I think
of the poetry

of Rene Char
and all he must have seen
and suffered
that has brought him
to speak only of
sedgy rivers,
of daffodils and tulips
whose roots they water,
even to the free-flowing river
that laves the rootlets
of those sweet-scented flowers
that people the
milky
way .

I remember Norma
our English setter of my childhood
her silky ears
and expressive eyes.
She had a litter
of pups one night
in our pantry and I kicked
one of them
thinking, in my alarm,
that they
were biting her breasts
to destroy her.

I remember also
a dead rabbit

lying harmlessly
on the outspread palm
of a hunter's hand.
As I stood by
watching
he took a hunting knife
and with a laugh
thrust it
up into the animal's private parts.
I almost fainted.

Why should I think of that now?
The cries of a dying dog
are to be blotted out
as best I can.
Rene Char
you are a poet who believes
in the power of beauty
to right all wrongs.
I believe it also.
With invention and courage
we shall surpass
the pitiful dumb beasts,
let all men believe it,
as you have taught me also
to believe it.

~William Carlos Williams

This poem reminds me of my own, more concrete experiences: A big brother, with the intent of scaring a tiny Shit-tzu of a dog, lobs a softball high into the air. When the plopping softball hurtles to the earth very near an unsuspecting consciousness the ensuing hilarity of scared-tiny-dog should be all that is required on a lazy summer evening before dinner. However, the skull-crushing projectile of intended hilarity comes a-plopping directly on tiny dog's head. The shock arrests his breath, his eyes gape, what will happen? Tiny dog straightens a rear leg out in a sort of bounding way, but there is no bounding, and the leg keeps stretching back- most unnaturally back. With a sort of twitch to the right tiny dog begins convulsing. A flurry of shouts and confusion bring a car to drive tiny dog to the veterinarian. I stroke the fur and mutter incomprehensible soothing into a tiny dog's ear as it convulses into rigid death.

That seems alot like life: a big joke intent on passing the time away crushing our skulls so that we may convulse our way to rigid death. That pretty much sums it up, and *the cries of a dying dog are to be blotted out as best I can*. Although everything I remember Brueghel painting reminds me of the horror of a crying dog, I like the idea that 'the power of beauty might right all wrongs.' Yes, I think I'll hold on to that thought as I look for a job to distract myself from the hurtl-plopping softball of intended hilarity coming to put the final touches of 'reality' on this my erstwhile life.

XXVIII

In childhood, we once crouched before our teacher
Growing content, in time, with what he taught;
How does the story end? What happened to us?
We came like water, and like wind were gone.

BREEZE

It was a tired, empty, suburban apartment complex. It was safe. Nothing ever happened here. The people went to work, came home, watched television, and slept. Whatever else occurred was merely coincidence. As I stared at the hungry holes of the dryers, beckoning to be stuffed with laundry, I thought about the tedious, the boring, the everyday. "It's all so..." I thought. My eyes drifted over the dirty and yellowing cream paint caked fifteen layers thick on the crumbling bricks. Long, exposed tubes of florescence, like captured and meaningless moonlight, buzzed overhead; ineffectual and washed out by the daylight. The concrete floor was stained with puddles of overflow. Hundreds of rings of long evaporated water were etched into its memory. Great hardened clumps of spider web, dust, and the sweaty oil of existence clogged every corner and crack. Pipes running in all directions were shellacked to the wall with an abundance of that same sickly cream-colored paint. I wondered what sorts of filth and fossil were trapped beneath the many layers—a twisted modern archaeology.

An abandoned strand of spider web was raised by the breeze, and I followed it with my eyes until it reached a tiny blue hand. More amazingly the blue hand was attached to a little blue man about two feet tall floating weightlessly at the end of the web. I stiffened with fear and adrenaline. The blue man had scary features: sharp black eyes, pointed white teeth, narrow opaque fingernails, and dark black hair trimmed to harsh angles. He was wearing a dark blue knee-length robe over dark blue genie pants and black slippers. Around his waist was a black rope knotted around crystals and silver discs. He wore an amber colored jewel mounted in a gold oval, about the size of a half-dollar, tied around his head so that it stuck firmly to his forehead. I thought of fleeing, but there was something in his grin that held me. He knew everything I was thinking and feeling, I guessed, and would know everything that was about to happen.

His expression was mischievous and mirthful. He pointed a sharp finger at me and said, "You want to make a journey, but you don't want to leave the room." Oh, was he wrong about that. Not only did I loathe that laundry room, the addition of his presence was making it more disagreeable than ever. Yet, I did not want to correct him. He continued, "You always know I'm here, but you never find me!" I tried to think of what to say to this, but nothing made sense. I remained dumb. He finally asked me, "What do you want?"

As if completing a thought I had begun earlier, I said, "I want life to make sense."

His eyes narrowed and his grin widened exposing even more of his frighteningly pointed teeth. "And what do you suppose I would have to do to you in order to render the universe sensible?" His voice rose and fell seeming both shrill and deep.

"I wouldn't think you'd have to do anything but show me." I answered trying to make it clear I wanted nothing 'done' to me.

"Then what do you want?" he repeated.

"Understanding," I said.

"Then shall I take you? Show you? Transform you?" His eyes glistened with knowing. He leered like a game show host teasing a contestant choosing between certain death and the big cash prize.

"What will happen to me?" I asked.

"You will be given that for which you ask," he replied.

"But what!" I said urgently, "What will you do with me?"

"Anything you ask," he repeated.

"Don't make me into anything I'm not," I warned him.

His lips quivered emitting the tiniest squeak of a laugh, "So it shall be." He let go of the floating web strand, and the breeze lifted him up like a balloon. It blew him into a wisp of blue smoke that sailed right through the wall and disappeared. I shook my head and rubbed my eyes, grappling with the reality of what had happened.

"Come back," I ventured feebly, "Are you coming back?" I began to feel ridiculous.

The dryer buzzed, and my no-longer-spinning clothes called to me for care and attention, but I could not give it. My mind drifted to my apartment of responsibilities, then to my family and all the people I knew and loved. I thought about my life—all the memories and feelings that would be lost with me if I was not careful. "One does have a certain responsibility to oneself," I thought, "and there's a fine line between adventure and foolishness." I could see my hungry fish and thirsty plants. The heavy images of a thousand concerns pulled my eyes out of focus. Then I remembered the first thing the blue man had said to me—You want to make a journey, but you don't want to leave this room. My folly fell upon me like a tub of water. What opportunities had I given up? I felt confused and deathly alone. An endless horizon of the grayest sea pushed against a leaden and sinking sky.

I don't know how long I sat in that room; it might have been days. My clothes had long since stopped spinning and had altogether lost any meaning. I didn't even go home. I walked out the door of that laundry room and kept walking. I never turned back. But in my memory, I can vaguely recall a little voice whispering, "Just in time."

LXXXI

Mysteries broached with joy in tavern talk
Have far more substance than a mumbled prayer
To you, my Last and First, my soul's Creator
Empowered either to sear or succor me.

SLEEP LIST

Did you remember your sleep list?

Sleep list?

You write down everything you need to remember so that you don't forget.

It's sleep!

Yeah?

So, you don't need a list. Your body and mind take care of things naturally. You relax – You sleep. No list required; in fact, I imagine it would interfere.

These are the voices I hear in a conversation it would seem I'm having with myself. In one of those tricks that apply mostly to the mentally challenged, and by that I mean all manner of high-functioning psychopaths as well, I seem to have developed a rather seasoned ability to have serious two-part conversations, arguments really, with myself.

I imagine that all people play with this dialogical thinking on occasion, perhaps when they are trying to reason through a problem or examine both sides of an issue. Though I suspect it remains a hypothetical adventure in what could qualify as a conversation — perhaps even emerge as a conversation— if had with the right person. Such things never seem to go as we prognosticate.

> *Not even a list of... of... things you want to dream?*
>
> *That might be interesting, but it is not what you were talking about. Sleep list! Stupid. A list of things to do tomorrow, maybe. But that's just a list, not a sleep list. Really? A list of things to remember for sleep?*

The real issue arises when these voices take on qualities. This might range from full-blown multi-personality disorder to unfocused conversations with imaginary people. Though, I've always been of the school that teaches "Just because you can't see it, doesn't mean it's not there." I'm still working with the relatively acceptable voices that I imagine as my mind taking on different speaking roles.

> *Maybe for just a second, I thought it would be helpful to have a list of... yeah. I guess that's just for other things. We have so many lists*

now. I'm going to need a list of lists just to keep track!

It's scary sometimes when one of those voices has an exceptionally moronic suggestion like, "*Did you remember your sleep list.*" The more a participant in your mental conversation comes across mentally challenged, the harder it is to accept that it's all you. While one does not have to *hear* different voices to write different voices, I wonder if being better at 'hearing' them speak in the mind's eye makes one better at expressing unique ways for them to communicate on the page. Maybe a good subtitle for this would be *The Fine Line Between Art & Madness*.

LIX

Those dupes of intellect and logic die
In arguments on being and not being;
Go ignoramus, choose your vintage well—
From dust like theirs grow none but unripe grapes.

OZPERLOO

There was a village, or perhaps they were better considered a small group of associated families, that governed themselves in a most peculiar way. Each adult member of the group was able to be king for one day. The next day, despite the orders of the previous king, the subsequent person in line would take the position. Perhaps the word *king* with its implications of divinity and masculinity wasn't as accurate as supreme ruler. Besides, all Ozperloons felt like they were God's Children. Only the most heinous crimes—the Big Three in most religions: Kill, Steal, Bear False Witness (i.e. don't)—could interfere with a person having their day as ruler.

Of course, difficulties did abound in the beginning. The people who hadn't thought through the full ramifications tended to act self-interestedly. A great deal of "ordering" things back-n-forth occurred before situations got rolling. On the plus side, not that many people were eligible to rule at first, so a person could expect to get at least one day of rule in a calendar year – if not two.

Nevertheless, it took a few years before most of the citizens realized that time spent in any kind of celebration of the day was time lost to answering the serious questions Ozperloons needed answered. It appears they were a swift bunch or the state of affairs an effective teacher, as they quickly understood the debilitation of shortsightedness. Combined with their method of self-rule, these realizations led rapidly to a deeply engrained form of Kantian "Categorical Imperative[1]".

Their concept of governance grew to include a simple and direct expectation of themselves to answer upcoming questions in a way that would be fair to everyone involved and not lead to the least bit of expectation that anyone else would overturn the decision (or at least to the slightest possible bit). Of course, they relied on other forms of guidance as well, such as the judiciary and their "documentation" or list of rights.

It is amazing what happened in the end. At some point, the group grew so prosperously and in such congruity that when their population exceeded the

---

[1] In broad strokes, the Categorical Imperative is the belief that any decision good for oneself must be good for all mankind under similar conditions.

number required to expect to be king for a day once, even in a lifetime, the people still prepared for the likelihood of rule. They seemed to completely internalize the concept of "the best for everyone" and bring it into their home lives. The unnecessary pomp and circumstance of being in power or becoming in power were all but abandoned. People participated in groups that worked towards understanding and solving problems, whether or not any in their group would ever serve.

It is true to recall that there was one time of year when they celebrated their accomplishments. They particularly celebrated the fact that many of the companies and organizations within Ozperloo had adopted this same means of governance. They called it *One Day*. They celebrated to remind themselves that they were all different individuals sharing a common space and giving each other the most room possible to enjoy their individuality. They did it so many different ways it would be nearly impossible to describe, but all the celebrations shared the same core theme. It's hard to tell if it's cornier than any of the other days they celebrated for various other reasons, but that day was undoubtedly the big one in their society.

It is also unclear if it would be possible to allow for such lessons on a modern stage. If the inhabitants hadn't gone through the period of time where they were overturning each other's selfishness, would the society itself have grown into the egalitarian place where each trusted the other to make the fairest choice? Would it have ever evolved such that each person could go his or her whole life without ever becoming King and still not really care about it, as everyone else was trusted to be prepared and fair just as the individual was? So many Ozperloons took their day so seriously and did their jobs with such attention to detail, it changed the way they saw themselves and others.

Maybe all candidates who wish to serve a country such as this one should be required to study for a few years in an Ozperloon model so that they come to this realization before accepting office. Plus, studying something for a few years before jumping in and selling their decisions couldn't hurt.

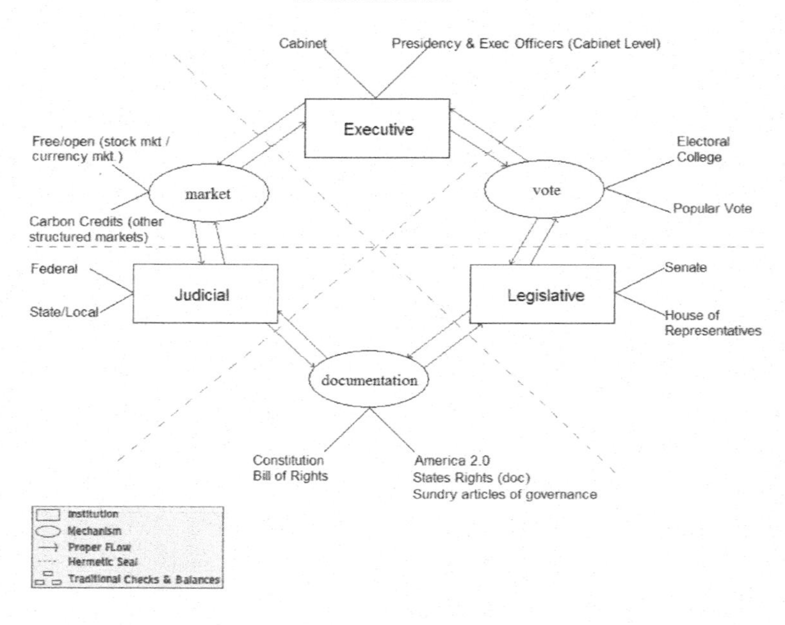

America 2.0 takes the old "checks & balances" of the three institutions and interweaves them with the three mechanisms. Each Institution and Mechanism is divided into popular and structured parts and hermetic seals are drawn across the schema: i.e. the Executive Branch should have no ability to change or defy the documentation (Constitution, Bill of Rights, etc.). The Judicial Branch should not interfere with the vote and the Legislative branch should not interfere with the open market. To keep the market from influencing the Legislative branch, limits to the amount of money that can be spent campaigning should be enacted as well as national term limits. Cabinet members should serve two-year terms, and only be replaced by the

President when the term is up. Though no appointments should be made in the last year of a presidency and if they were they should count as open seats. This should dilute our current us/them bipartisan struggle.

XXXI

In agitation I was brought to birth
And learned nothing from life but wonder at it;
Reluctantly we leave still uninformed
Why in the world we came, or went, or were.

NEO-FRIVOLISM

Well, this is not at all what I expected – how like life? I was repositioning some of my detritus, which had become strewn about the globe (at least the western U.S.) like so many dead flower petals, and I came across this book in a ski bag. I had heard neither of the book nor the author. However, I felt a sort of 'tingle' or subconscious urge to read it. I found it slow going the first thirty pages or so and probably took three months to finish. At the end, however, I had a kind of epiphany about myself and some of my 'johnist' thoughts. This feeling was accentuated when I read the following (last two) paragraphs of the *Translator's Afterword*. Without going into it much further, I found a need to share them.

First however, since I think it's unlikely anyone reading this will have read the book, it is somewhat important to summarize - as briefly as possible - the plot, so that the following observations have some context or background. The short novel (170 softcover pages) is called *Oliver VII* by Antal Szerb. I'd be very curious to know how many people have heard of the book or author. I hadn't and didn't even imagine the date it was written –let alone how it got into my ski bag.

In short, very short, it is about a king (Oliver VII) of a fictional eastern-European nation-state, who impersonates a "Nameless Captain" in order to participate in overthrowing his own regime. Once completed, he relocates to Venice and falls in with con-people as a somewhat ordinary Oscar from South America. He also falls "in love" with Marcelle a beautiful but common girl on the team who thinks him somewhat a simpleton. (The natural result of 'royalty' in ordinary circumstances, I wonder?) As things develop, it turns out he and this gang become engaged in a scheme to have Oscar impersonate Oliver VII –the deposed king to whom he bears a striking resemblance. Then an opportunity presents itself for him to do some 'real good' (as it were) for his country / countrymen, but only if he will give up the charade of the charade and really return to being king. He does this; however, he is no longer able to maintain his relationships with the "gang" now that he is king. He thought he would and went as far as making them ministers of this or that. He had learned, after all, what it was to be a king from these guys telling him what an idiot and how "un-kinglike" he was. Then, when he became king again, he learned yet more about what it means to be a person in a "role" of sorts... or to be a person in a class? Perhaps it's best to say only: to be a person whose personhood is reflected as much or more by the milieu into which he or she was born (or self-identified) – and give it no more basis in "reality" than that? I'm not sure in the end, but that's what the book is about in VERY, VERY condensed terms.

This moved me, but it was all-the-more intensified when I read about the author and his life in the aforementioned afterword by the translator. But before I go on to what all this meant to me, let me go through the semi-arduous (can't I just scan it?) task of retyping these last two paragraphs I've discussed:

> *Oliver VII, then, far from a mere afterthought to Szerb's more 'significant' novels, is a source of new understanding of them. Indeed it is only when the three novels are taken together that the prevailing spirit of his art can be fully understood. Over the eight years his values have not so much changed as clarified, and Oliver VII is in some ways their most direct expression. The 'neo-frivolism' alluded to in Pendragon can now be seen as the subtle business it is. Szerb nowhere expands this concept into a formal philosophy—that would hardly have been in the spirit—but its implications are many and various. Its essence*

was caught by the religious historian Károly Kerényi, who said of the writer that "he never took himself seriously." This was more than a compliment; it exactly reflected the value Szerb attached to the 'self' as in 'self-interested' and 'self-important'. If personality is plural—as Freud, and Pirandello, knew,
and Pendragon wittily demonstrated—then the different selves that make it up will include some very odd bedfellows. For Szerb's mentors, if that is what they were, the consequences are potentially tragic: reality is unknowable, and the poor battered ego is locked into a hopeless struggle for stability. Szerb turns that conclusion on its head. [so does johnism] *Since life, for him, is a joyous miraculous thing, and love not entirely an illusion, the instability of the 'self' is in fact a form of release. Its inconsistent nature, and the endlessly ingenious strategies it devises to keep its end up,*
are necessarily comic. The art that grows from this realization is too benign for satire, too shrewd for sentimentality; it pulls off that almost impossible trick of accommodating a disillusion bordering on cynicism with an amused, indeed delighted, acceptance of the world with all its faults. Its origins may lie as much in Szerb's religious predisposition as in any psychological theory, but the message it sends out was not a bad one for its time.

In October 1942, the questions of identity and loyalty that feature so strongly in Szerb's fiction took a new and urgent form. A lifelong Catholic and a sincere if somewhat free-thinking Christian, he found himself reclassified as a Jew (by descent) and therefore an alien in the land of his birth. Religious affiliation was no longer a defense. Now it was his turn to choose: between living out the role he had been so cruelly allotted, and the chance to flee. At first he simply clung to hope, while his scholarly works were banned, and Oliver VII, passed off as a translation from the English of a supposed A H Redcliff, sank without trace (his widow kept it in a drawer for the next twenty years). He lost the right to teach in his university and was summoned for periods of forced labor. Next came the yellow star and the ghetto. Ahead lay the death camps. He was presented with repeated opportunities to escape; someone arranged an academic post for him at Columbia University. Each time he sadly but firmly declined. Some of those close to him, such as the poet Agnes Nemes Nagy, thought he acted from naïve optimism, misplaced idealism, or the misguided notion that his fame as a scholar and writer gave him exemption; and those factors may have played some part. But there was also a real commitment to Hungary and his work there ("How can I teach students who haven't read their Vörösmarty?"); and, even more, an unshakeable loyalty to those he loved. In 1944 he was officially granted permission to emigrate, but stayed because the Arrow Cross threatened reprisals against his wife. Similarly, just weeks before his horrific death in January 1945, he rejected help because his younger brother was in the same camp. On another occasion, he simply refused to leave if it meant abandoning his old colleagues and friends Gábor Halász and György Sárközy. (It made no difference. They survived not much longer than he did.) Friends wrote of the 'mood of resignation' that came over him, and the way he continued to put others first, to think of their needs when his own prospects were becoming so dark. It is impossible not to connect these attitudes with the values enshrined in his books, not least Oliver VII. Indeed, almost all the qualities that made Antal Szerb such a remarkable human being seem to find expression in his radiantly benign last novel. ~ *Len Rix / August 2007*

The underlines and bracketed parts are mine. I couldn't help wonder if one is more constrained to die, as Don Quixote might only understand, in the name of a fiction that should be, as opposed to a reality that might be? Or, if reality is nothing more than that which we invent as such, if making the ultimate sacrifice for THAT truth, is really all there is... (it is, by some definitions, all that there is—it is your 'johnism'). Without which, what – the sine qua non of one's very existence – to sacrifice that fiction for survival? Hmm. What must it be like to be offered freedom from a death camp, but at the expense of leaving your brother or other loved one behind? Needless to say, this whole book makes me think to no end, in my ever-more-circular (ahhh) wheel-of-thought.

I confess to having been very excited to look up "neo-frivolity" in Wikipedia, as I was unaware of it as a literary trope. Perhaps there was a whole genre of which I was unaware? At any rate, I was surprised to find that the word doesn't exist, nor does frivolity itself as a literary term/genre/movement. I probably needn't add that I have adopted a sort of hopeful self-inclusion, "I might want to be a neo-frivolist!" Indeed, I might want to be a member of any literary meme that doesn't exist. Antal Szerb, Len Rix, myself, other's –anyone? get 'em!

I was also new to the idea that the normal personality might include multiple forms, as, I gather, Freud and Pirandello were not. Alas, though, if the 'self' or 'reality' or 'religion' is indeed, as johnism would have it, merely a creation of your own POV, than why not more than one? It is not as if we are predisposed to monism, ask any good Hindu. The wealth of gods and goddesses from ancient times until now clearly reflect how much my intrinsically "monist" johnism was formed by a Lutheran (at least religiously) education. And though I can contemplate a plurality of imagined personality, I still struggle against the thought that there isn't a dominant or most-'true' fiction (reality) or 'johnism'... hmmm, how I enjoy thinking of johnism as the pre-eminent fiction in a host of competing weltanschauungen.

The translator also writes, "...reality is unknowable..." and "...love is not entirely an illusion..." I really didn't know there were other people dwelling on this topically apparent catch-22 of lucidity. And it made me think about implications of johnism I've expounded such as "love, money, and time aren't real." They are what we focus most of our lives on pursuing, but they aren't 'real', as such, they are ideas. But are they "entirely an illusion"? Well, not in so far as they can be part of your johnism or 'ultimate created reality'. As far as everything is imagined, yes, but as far as that which we imagine is the only thing that is real, they hold fast to some semblance of truth. If they are a part of everyone's imagined reality, then there is some commonality or shared experience to that. Again, hmmmm.

Then there is the post- *Death: or The Playground*[2] part, where I keep saying be careful what you wish for (or write/think about). For no sooner is a certain belief system out of your head, then you can bet depraved fortuna some sort of test of that 'truth' is headed your way. If you claim to know about life after death, well nine out of ten times...

And to think this was published in Hungarian back in 1942 only to spend twenty years in a drawer, and for this English translation to surface in 2007? -talk about the Van Gogh Principle[3] in action. And then somehow (though some would say unsurprisingly) to find its way into my ski bag... not my doing! Well, I suppose it means that just when you think carrying on in your madness has taken you far enough (not far enough, too far), the universe will send some your way. As John Irving put it, "Keep passing open windows!" As John Cady put it, "Neo-Frivolists unite!"

---

[2] *Death: or The Playground* is a play written and produced by John Cady & David Jamison in 2004.

[3] The Van Gogh Principle essentially juxtaposes the painter's life spent in extreme poverty unable to give away his work with the current values of his paintings—in the millions if not 100's of millions of dollars. In a sentence: Monetary reward, or socio-political reward/fame during lifetime is not the surest sign an artist or politician is doing the right thing.

RETROCAST

Retrocast also **Retrocasted |Retrocasting** (v.): \'re-(ˌ)trō-kast\ To use the current situation – e.g. fame, money, success, or power – to predict how an unknown past might have seemed, or to use an outcome to determine the meaning and impact of the precedent. It often contains the *cum hoc ergo propter hoc* fallacy, or the confusion of coincidence / correlation with causality.

It is the heretofore nonexistent antonym to **forecast** (or **forecasted | forecasting**), explaining the human obsession with predicting how the past would have occurred to one using the wisdom of hindsight.

THE SYSTEM IS BROKEN

Part 1: Impossible

This dive into the bowels of the "the system", for me, begins when I got a ticket while at an audition in the MTV building near the Water Garden. It was May. I was only about 15 minutes past my meter expiration, but that was enough time for the fast-acting troops of the Department of Parking Enforcement to have written their request for $45.00 of penance in association with this violation of the norms of social conduct. This, our city elders deem, is fair treatment. Though it's hard to find twenty minutes in the middle of an audition to walk out from a multi-story building and feed the meter, and auditions notoriously run late. Well, "That's the way the cookie crumbles," as-they-say, though I don't know why—so, I wrote a check and got on with my life.

Several weeks later I received a letter from the City of Los Angeles Department of Parking Enforcement. They would like me to know that a ticket they had recently issued to me was not paid within 21-days, and I would therefore be required to pay a late charge amounting to more than the original penalty.

Despite the fact that I had paid this $45.00 ticket, they now wanted $110.00! I was sure I had paid, but also realized mistakes are sometimes made. I rationalized, "These things often cross in the mail." I checked my bank account online and sure enough the check had cleared. I ignored the letter.

Weeks later, I received another letter informing me that the unpaid amount would soon be sent to a collection agency and that the mere fact of its having been sent there would be sure to have an adverse effect on my credit rating. I printed out a copy of the cancelled check from my online account and a copy of my transaction history wherein I highlighted the transaction in question. I sent this to the City of Los Angeles Department of Parking Enforcement (hereafter ~ CLADPE) along with a letter explaining to them that I had already paid the ticket in question.

In a few weeks, I received a letter from CLADPE stating that they would not be able to look into my situation at all until I sent them a photocopy of the cancelled check itself. I sighed. Already, this was becoming tedious. I was "in the system" by virtue of 15 minutes of parking, and it appeared they were going to make it as difficult as possible to get out even if I had already paid. I undertook to secure my cancelled check, I drove to Kinkos, I photocopied the check, I drove home, I wrote another letter, I bought stamps, I mailed the photocopy with a letter requesting that they check their records to see that the ticket in question was paid and, in turn, not deliver me to the collectors and inflict life-altering damage upon my credit score.

In a few weeks, I received a letter from CLADPE stating that they would not be able to look into my situation at all until I sent them a photocopy of BOTH SIDES of my cancelled check. I sighed. All they would really have to do is check their records and see that my ticket had been paid, but no, instead of any checking on their part, there would be "proving" on my part. Though there are many factors contributing to the "brokenness" of the system, this is a key component.

I drove to Kinko's, I photocopied BOTH SIDES of my cancelled check, I drove home, I wrote another letter requesting that they look into my situation: "To Whom It May Concern, In regard to ticket number xxxxxxx7895. I have already paid this with check #2419 on 5/25 etc., please see enclosed copies of my cancelled check." I relaxed.

In a few weeks, I received a letter from CLADPE. They wished to inform me that I was right. They had indeed received my payment, and I should disregard all letters to the contrary – they would not be turning me over to the collection agency.

A few days later, I received another letter from CLADPE reminding me that they were going to send my ticket to the collection agency, but I merely grinned at the funny system that doesn't seem to know what it is or is not doing at any given moment and threw the letter away.

In a few weeks, I received a letter from a collection agency. They were interested in informing me that the ticket for which I had not paid the city of Los Angeles had subsequently been turned over to them. There were many things they could do to me, in addition to the adverse effects they were already visiting upon my credit score, but it would be in everyone's best interest if I would simply relinquish the one hundred and ten dollars that I now owed them, and which they were anxious to have. I wrote letters, I made calls, I drove to Kinko's, I photocopied checks. It didn't matter.

**An important piece of advice to anyone who makes the grievous trip to Kinko's to photocopy cancelled checks: make SEVERAL copies of BOTH SIDES. Don't just make one copy and trust in your ability to sort out* *the problem with a well-crafted letter. The copies are only about five cents each; you'll spend that much in gas driving back and forth for each of the several hundred times you're likely to have to resend information when dealing with CLADPE. I suggest 10 is a nice target for your first trip. Put the remaining 9 in a file, you'll be using them before you know it and you'll feel brilliant for having compensated for their incompetence.*

It became time to renew the registration on my car around December. I received a request from the DMV for the State of California for $370.00, which represented $260.00 to register my car and $110.00 for the ticket I had apparently declined to pay (which was currently in collections and adversely affecting my credit score). I sent the DMV $260.00 for my renewal, proof of insurance, and a note explaining that the ticket they had included had been paid with check #2419 along with references numbers regarding my ongoing correspondence with CLADPE. In a few weeks, I received a letter from the DMV announcing that I had not "fully paid" for my registration on time. Therefore I was being assessed a $149.00 late fee, so that I now owed them an additional $259.00 because the first $110.00 of my $260.00 had been given to a collection company for a ticket. The ticket I had already paid. So they required the $110.00 I had shortchanged them on my registration and an additional $149.00 for their trouble (ostensibly due to the $260.00 being late, though it was sent on time with explanations). A quick look at the math: $45.00 for 15 minutes, plus $65.00 for being late (though I had paid) + $149.00 for late registration = $259.00 on top of the legitimate $260.00 + $45.00 for a grand total of $564.00 (when they paid the collection agency $110.00, they effectively repaid my initial $45.00). I'm now out $259.00, because the system is broken and no one cares.

I called them. Finally, someone on the other end of the phone was bright enough to inform me that, though I had paid a ticket on time. There was ANOTHER ticket, which hadn't been paid. But I did not receive "ANOTHER" ticket, I told her. Nevertheless, there it was, there was a different ticket with a different number in their records. The check I had spent all this time photocopying was for a different ticket. Whew! That was helpful... at least there was some sense in the world. I asked how I might dispute the ticket that I didn't get. There was nothing I could do, she said, because I hadn't disputed the ticket within 60 days. I told her I didn't know there was a ticket to dispute, and that in fact I had disputed it by sending a letter saying I had paid the ticket (and by implication all tickets I was aware of). But she assured me there was nothing she could do, and that I would not get my registration until I paid the outstanding balance. I asked why no one there was smart enough to read my letter saying, "In regards to ticket number xxxxxxx7895, I have already paid this..." and reply, "No, you paid ticket number xxxxxxx4127 with check #2419 and you have not paid ticket number xxxxxxx7895." But surely, she understood that my letter claiming to have paid all known tickets was my way of disputing any tickets I had not paid? No, there was nothing she could do. It had been more than 60 days and she thanked me for my time.

I gave up. I threw in the towel. You can't beat **the system**. It doesn't care (they who comprise it do not care). So I paid the extra $259 and waited for my registration. It never came.

XIV

The rose cried: ‘I am generous of largesse
And laughter. Laughingly my petals blow
Across the world; the ribbons of my purse
Snap and its load of coin flies everywhere’.

BECKY & TODD

(touched)

The car in front of him did not move. There was no apparent reason for this auto-intransigence, and this was exactly the kind of thing that happened when he was late. "This is exactly the kind of 'minor miracle' that illustrates my point about the universe," he thought. Though he was never entirely sure what that point was, and it varied more frequently than even he suspected.

And this is Todd: steaming, fuming, honking, wondering what the hell goes through people's minds when they behave this way. It's hard to be a 'man on a mission' in a world full of people who have nothing better to do than stare at road signs and wonder what they mean and why there are so many of them. As the aging beige sedan before him sputtered around the corner, Todd greased the pavement with his rear tires to send a clear message about his frustration. He wasn't sure if the woman would 'get it' but it made him a little happier nonetheless.

As he breezed down the road, it did not occur to him that there was really no reason for him to hurry.

Anywhere worth going was worth going quickly, right? So Todd sped, and smiled, and enjoyed the rush of buildings and cars and trees and other objects he was whooshing by. "Whooshing" –if there was a word that described the joy Todd got out of driving, that would be it. It wasn't a word he'd use, but it was what he liked. Todd was a whoosher.

Becky nudged her glasses into the perfect position—an act she repeated thousands of times each day. She retouched her handbag to affirm its presence and looked at all the people around her at the crosswalk. But she looked only shoulder level or below. Becky did not risk eye-contact lightly. She was wearing what would otherwise be considered a sharp office-suit arrangement, betrayed only by the quality of the material, which was suffused with polysynthetic petrochemical derivatives. If you looked at it and thought "K-Mart" you were overestimating.

Becky touched her glasses. Todd whooshed and thumped the base of his thumb on the steering wheel. The light turned yellow then red. The upheld hand blinked from forbidding red to an inviting blue-white figure of perambulation, people tensed and began to move. Becky stepped off the curb and WHOOOSH a bright red blur stretched by, nearly brushing her, and whistled through the intersection.

Though everything that had just happened was a blur to Becky, one thing remained frozen in time. On a fairly average day, walking a very traditional route, Becky had made eye contact with a stranger in a red car. It was unbelievable. Becky stood transfixed. All the other pedestrians crossed the street, but Becky stood there just off the curb. She didn't move. She played the moment over and over in her mind. Everything around her – the people's torsos, the shoes, legs, feet, her handbag, the red – was a rush of fuzzy detail, but right in the middle, as though someone had cleaned but a tiny circle in a dirty window, there were these eyes locked on hers. Suddenly, intimately, someone had just seen Becky for what she was—had really seen her. And was now blocks away, whistling, whooshing, and perhaps even completely unaware of what had just happened.

LXVII

They say, “be sober lest you die of drink
And earn Hell fire on God’s Last Judgment Day”
Nevertheless my blaze of drunkenness
Outshines both worlds, your now and your hereafter.

THE REVIEW

I think we are all now ready for the conversation. The point is fun and betting. Life is much more like being stuck in a *Library* than being a member of a book club. You can check out any book you want, but you can never leave.

I think it is perfectly accurate to point out that the author thinks he's much better off than he is. Yet somehow he, his endorsers, the would-be movie makers, and many others seem to have missed the sort of slapdash congruence of the object. That short snippet with his mother was so out of place in the book and simultaneously THE POINT – assuming there was one. I agree that the intention is to say something about the material (commercial) nature of our society often at the expense of our humanity or spirit, but we had arrived at this idea by page ten or so and find that nothing has been added or subtracted some hundred pages later. The argument seems to be a simple repetition of a semi-original juxtaposition. So, it would seem we agree to an extent on at least one of the major flaws. That is an odd thing to write about the work of someone so theoretically successful.

There are funny scenes and glimpses of meaning in the chapters, but so much seems a repurposing of articles that were formerly rejected by *Rolling Stone*. They've got to have a home at some point, no? It would be like me putting a bunch of emails into a book called, *eXistEntiAlasM.* Well, they do say that emulation is the sincerest form of flattery (and originality is not revealing your sources). Who knows, maybe the whole concept of this gathering warrants being coalesced into a book after a few more Superbowls (and victory parties).

But, back to the passages that were worth mentioning and how much fun we will have re-enacting them. The gratuitousness is another good point. Is ladling that treacle over previously cliché and one-note scenes what passes for commentary these days? Yes—you have to heighten your hero or point (or anti-hero in this case) in order for the audience to care about the sisyphean plunge (is Sisyphean Plunge the name of a band? If not, it should be). At the same time, we really must believe in this "fate" or the story fails. Compare it to the overwhelming over-the-topness of Mark Leyner or wild-ride and self-inclusion of Hunter S. Thompson and it becomes all too apparent (and now I'll unfairly lump all the writing into the 'I've-only-read-one' boat) that this entire oeuvre lacks (or is likely to lack) the element that makes us want more.

However, I don't think Leyner has had any films made, and the good Dr. notoriously hated (and embraced the shear madness of) Hollywood. Unlike the aforementioned, however, it would seem none of us have figured out how to survive in the glitter without "earning" our way to normalcy and mediocrity. Well, the Reverend has skirted the tails of that debutante in aligning with the almighty. One certainly can't make Thompsonian or Leynarian comparisons without dealing with what is not allowed and staking a claim for what is rightly divine (i.e. he does get to play to a "higher" audience, whether or not anyone cares to believe in any part of the ensemble).

To that end, I will allude no more to this collective immersion in reviewing this piece of glamour. It would be interesting to see what would have to happen to make us want yet more wit, but there is no argument that this is a polarizing figure. We love or hate; we think poseur or prophet, and there is undoubtedly some credit due there. Of course, Salman Rushdie got death threats for *The Satanic Verses* which has still not been cinematized. It, arguably, holds just as cursory a reign over real issues. Though, that might occur as the pot calling the kettle black to anyone reading this. Is the point more who you offend than what you actually say? I mean banning and death threats are the work of small minds and should not be substituted for strictly literary success. Neither should making the object d'art into cinema (or a film) for that matter, but our hive-think centralizes on Hollywood!

It has been speculated that we live in an age that does not accept satire. What? I cannot imagine? The nuanced relationship between parody, satire, and mockery is as crucial (or MORE) in this age. The post-structural nee deconstructed age is probably the high point of satire. If not here, where? If not now, when? On a personal note, I think that satire mocks the intent (seriously or otherwise), while parody mocks the thing itself or what Kant might call the "ding an sich." One might j'accuse this nonsense of being a satire of the parody that I've experienced as life. The surfaces, things, material itself stand in monetarily supported contrast to the spirit, soul, sensitivity, or compassion that we are supposed to witness. Is it absent, blocked, waiting behind the corner?

Actually, if we were told on page one that the main character would not change one iota by page four hundred, would we have read beyond thirty (or at all)? Or is the narrator's change the final acceptance of the fact that society is not going to incarcerate or indict him, or is it his final acceptance of his own weak will? But, it's not really that is it? He doesn't accept his fate (new fate?) so much as bravely accept his own apathy? But, bravely or not, the acceptance of his own apathy was where he started. He didn't need a murderous rampage in order to discover that he was apathetic. By doing so, he only continually points out his own indictment of society for doing so and doing so, and on, and still... I'm sure the author meant that HIS story is THE story, but I can't seem to believe that his story didn't start and end AS clichéd, simple, one-note, unevolved, AS the society he seemingly denigrates. In the end it comes off like staring for six weeks in a mirror to prove a point.

XXXVIII

Yesterday in the market stood a potter
Pounding relentlessly his batch of clay.
My inner ear could hear it sigh and groan:
'Brother, I was once like you. Treat me gently!'

WHY TEENS LOVE VAMPIRES

Why are teens today so fascinated with vampire myth? Whether in books, TV, film, or online (including games), it appears vampirism is the hottest outlet for the pubescent imagination. Could it be that the youth of today recognize in the Vampire-Ruling-Class (VRC) a dark reflection of modern society? As oil companies pour oil into the environment in Niger or the Gulf while posting record profits, and enormous international conglomerates hop in and out of bankruptcy or bailouts, and entire nations like Greece, Spain, Ireland, Italy, and Portugal teeter on the verge of insolvency, it appears more likely that the entire global monetary structure is a vast ponzi scheme that is intended to keep the owners of the top 1% of wealth right where they are.

The monarchy-ruling classes of yore learned the hard way that you can't keep a good peasant down long enough. They tended to lose their heads in popular revolutions. They eventually realized that the key, of course, is to let the peasant participate in the "democracy" of his or her own demise. As long as "a select few" are seen to break through to riches, the vast unwashed masses will *indenture themselves* to servitude and the yolk for a lifetime. Two important requirements must obtain: 1.) money needs to be realized as debt, so whenever people become too prosperous, the interest rate can be ratcheted up to keep the "rented capital" that makes the whole system function in the hands of the 1% (proportionally). 2.) failure must be seen as the fault of the individual, concurrently, some individuals must be allowed to come from the very bottom to the very top in order to perpetuate the self-responsibility / self-liberation illusion.

There are some aspects of modernity that serve as perfect examples of this "lottery" scenario (besides the lottery itself –aka: extra tax on the poor). Acting, professional sports, music, and sometimes even politics are excellent examples of the masses working for little or nothing (certainly sub-survival) in order to remain in contact with the slim chance of lottery-like dreams come true. A simple example is a successful restaurant that rents its physical property year over year. The more successful the restaurant, the higher the rent can be raised. As long as there is an abundance of individuals willing to try the restaurant business, the cycle can be repeated with restaurant after restaurant. As one grows popular the rent rises, then prices rise, people move on, and the restaurant goes bust. This is a common occurrence. Industry lore has it that 9/10 restaurants fail in the first year. According to *Business Week* 25% of restaurants fail in the first year, and 60% by five years. What might surprise one is that the 60% failure rate compares to the cross-industry average for all new businesses.

To extend the analogy to a world stage, one must only imagine that what is being rented out is the entire float of "debt" that powers the global economy. As more and more is produced and consumed, the 1% owning this float merely adjusts the interest so that the bulk of wealth remains with the creators of money. Churn (be it in people, restaurants, companies, multi-nationals, or nations) is essential for the system to remain in place. There is not enough wealth in the world to pay back the entirety of wealth (created, invented, manufactured) plus interest. Thus, the entire system is dependent on scarcity and competition. What the market really "fixes" is a kind of starvation point. Ideally, there are enough people willing to trade their lives for the means of survival long enough to support a small luxury, or ownership, or rentier class (VRC). Many people are competing to get into this class, but the vast majority are simply part of the churn that must (by force of the structure of the system) get by at near-subsistence wages. It has to be so, or too many people would either A.) save too much money and therefore stop working or B.) die from too much lack / overexertion / starvation. What the "free-enterprise" system does is 'set' this subsistence wage, or value, and keep the majority, "the food", in that position – alive, but not too prosperous. If one keeps slaves, one is forced to feed, clothe, and provide health care to keep them alive and working. If one creates a system that effectively exchanges the bulk of the slave's productive time on earth in a "voluntary" exchange for subsistence wages, then one can leave them to forage for their own food and medical care, and discard them altogether when they are no longer productive.

It is essential not to confuse the word "slave" with the type of racism that is freshly on the minds of most Americans. All peoples of all types and colors have enslaved one another throughout history. The word slave should not conjure the image of African Americans, but rather that of the "people" required by one group in order to perpetuate their way of living.

Is this not similar to the modern vampire ethos? Where early vampires were evil (if slightly charismatic), often tortured, misshapen, sometimes sickly looking, and confined to the night; modern vampires have negotiated the daylight, are perpetually twenty, and preternaturally beautiful. They are usually wealthy and extremely powerful, physically and psychologically, on top of being immortal. If bothered by anything, it is a vague sense of anxious schadenfreude or ennui regarding their great burden. Oh, they still suck the blood of their human "food". Why is the myth sexy, seductive, attractive? Because, every so often, a human isn't just eaten; he or she is selected to be given the boon of this immortal power. If no one ever had a chance at becoming a vampire, and we were all perpetually doomed to being their food, would anyone find them interesting at all? They would be the archenemy with whom we would engage in terrible battle for survival at the top of the food chain or at whose hands we would face permanent enslavement. They would be utterly repulsive to mortal, soulful humanity.

However, add to the mix that every so often they will take some "chosen" individual from our vast unwashed masses and share with them the gift of being in the top 1% (or NOT FOOD), and then everything is OK. Modern unrestrained capitalism, built upon the bedrock of debt issued by banks and rented at a rate that ensures its stability, is exactly the same as vampirism. It is Vampire-Capitalism; what an ironic acronym VC turns out to be.

Look at our most popular form of entertainment: *American Idol*. The basic element of this show is watching our fellow humans fail at the attempt to transcend their 'unchosen' state. If we can say that humans don't like being food, slaves, or even serfs (ask the monarchy), this show proves that humans do love being better humans than their fellow humans in the celebrated lottery of modern vampire-capitalism. Watching fellow citizens reach for the golden ring and fail, and humiliate themselves, and be *far worse than you*, brings the lotto ethos to the living room... WITH SINGING!

It seems like the youngest generation, the generation after Generation Y (Why?) or The Millennials, sometimes called generation Z or GenTech sees this situation. They don't seem to care if it's fair or not. They don't seem to care how it got this way or if it can be fixed. They just want to know if they're vampires or food. And it's a little hard not to sympathize with the choice they are imagining for themselves... given the options.

CX

Though pearls in praise of God I never strung,
Though dust of sin lies clotted on my brow:
Yet will I not despair of mercy.
When did Omar argue that one was two?

MY WAR

I am fighting a war. As with all wars, it is primarily with myself. There is a cast of characters. There is a setting. There is even an enemy – of course there is – there has to be. As this war is fought, it is accompanied by the struggle to maintain the illusion of this enemy. As it always seems to be, as I grow tired, as I let go, the enemy dissolves. The war fades to grey, and I am alone. In this space, I understand that it is only with myself that I make war.

In time, however, I am able to reinvent the enemy and strike up the band. It is terrible. While it is no Dresden, Hiroshima, or My Lai, it is my battle. To jump from this battle to those is only to change the characters, the setting, the intensity of the horror. Battle-hardened veterans will laugh, will sigh, will know what only they can know, but if they quiet their minds, they will feel this truth – their truth. The hardest battles they fought did not involve bombs or bullets, but were – as is mine – with themselves, with their minds – bodies – souls.

I am humbled by the wars others have fought—fiercer, bloodier, more epic than my own. This, in the end, is only my story. It is my war with myself, with fate, with reality, with existence. These are the characters, this is the setting, as with so many other war stories it ends in birdsong or with butterflies. It begins with love; it ends with love...like all war...like all stories...like all life.

XXXII

My presence here has been no choice of mine;
Fate hounds me most unwillingly away.
Rise, wrap a cloth about your loins, my Saki
And swill away the misery of this world.

SUFFERING

The trick is there is nothing to do - nothing that can be done. Eastern mystics have long said something along these lines: "cessation of desire". But even that is not something for which one can "hanker" –as it were, even desiring to be absent of desire is a desire. As suggested in Dzogchen[4], everything is already perfect in its entirety.

The discussion of perfection, whether traced back to Baruch Spinoza or Dzogchen, will reflect nothing but what we see in passing any artifact of natural or human creation. If, in it, you are able to see that the very act of perceiving exposes you to the billions of brilliant lights composing the universe, you have access to the perfection, the wholeness, the totality. But, can this become an impediment to doing anything at all?

I don't think the point is the cessation of action, but rather the idea that it makes a difference. This calls to mind the expression, "Chop wood, carry water." That which we do without desire or attachment to

[4] Dzogchen is a sect of Tibetan Buddhism.

the outcome is neutral and could almost be said to be guided by a divine hand, to the degree such a thing can be imagined – Tat Tvam Asi[5]!

Donovan expresses something like this in his song "There Is A Mountain," reflecting another favorite of eastern philosophy, *"first there is a mountain, then there is no mountain, then there is."* I believe the source material tries to say something like,

> When we first interact with the world we are confronted with mountains and rivers that block our way. Later, when we begin to master the techniques of enlightenment, we conquer these obstacles and find there are no mountains or rivers. However, once we have mastered enlightenment, we find that there are once again mountains and rivers (only they do not block our path since we are not going anywhere).

---

[5] Phrase used in Vedantic philosophy that translates roughly as "That Thou Art" or "You Are It" – implying parts or all of the self and the eternal are one.

It seems the point is that we have accepted our role in perfection and no longer have any need to overcome obstacles.

If one accepts this line of thinking, then how does desire arise? If one is perfectly a part of the perfection that is the totality of the universe, then mustn't one's "desire" also be perfectly a part of this as well? If it is derived from an "illusion" of separation, then this same illusion is part of the divine perfection. I'm sure it has occurred to most people contemplating this illusion that whether or not one chooses to suffer from it is of no significance. Thus, my suffering is of no importance to universal perfection or any illusion—divine, human, or otherwise.

However, why then the pledge to come back? Why the Boddhisattva or Tolku pledge to keep coming back until every soul is enlightened? It is illusion that we suffer, but the Dalai Lama would be quick to point out that there is also 'compassion'. It is probably important to have compassion even if it is *for* or *towards* an inevitable state of 'thusness' that is always going to be anyway. If it is not, how did this state of affairs come into being? Could it be argued that divine perfection accidentally found itself in a state (illusion/suffering) from which it now desires (no, there's that word again) to extricate itself? Can compassion really be understood as a wish to help every soul achieve escape from an illusion that the divine perfection deliberately chose? What sense of perfection accidentally stumbles into such an unfortunate state of being that it thereupon becomes concerned with extricating every reflection of the sexsexagintillion[6] diamonds in Indra's Web[7]?

Perhaps that seeming catch-22 arises because the answers to those questions are what Nagarjuna would have called the unknowables or inexpressibles. If in fact this is the case, we are returned to the original concept that this suffering is due to desire and must end with the cessation of desire, for no apparent reason whatsoever.

Ultimately, 'johnism' provides no superior solution to this conundrum. There is only that the existing approach seems to have stopped halfway. Let us agree to the premise that we exist in various states of desiring good and wishing to avoid suffering, but why

---

[6] A very large number, in this case a 1 with 201 zeroes following- the exact number isn't essential

[7] A Hindu/Buddhist analogy representing the universe as infinitely interconnected. Imagine a multi-dimensional web with a multifaceted diamond at each intersection reflecting all the other diamonds in the web.

limit ourselves to "chopping wood and carrying water." Of course, the phrase is merely an expression of doing those simple things required to survive, but why not build space shuttles, seek perpetual power sources, and invent religions that ease mankind's burden? The real question is whether or not the whole of existence can eventually be liberated from this state (this wheel of samsara). If it can, the simple life and the pledge of the Boddhisatva or Tolku makes sense. If not, why not simply embrace our suffering and tug at the giant chinese-finger-puzzle of life that this divine perfection has chosen to play. Even if we (one / any individual) did escape the wheel, it is unlikely that everyone will, and since there is no "independent you" to save, why bother trying? What assumptions have been made about the nature and essence of suffering? If it is inevitable, why don't we embrace the suffering and move on – or is this the same thing as eliminating desire?

It has been further suggested that any "eternity" one experiences is only a temporary condition. For anything to have meaning, such as a life, it must have its opposite or the "not it." For one to become, one must not have been, for the eternity to make any sense it too must cease at some point (a notion that undermines the meaning of the word). Some linguistic theory fits perfectly with the "bubbling universe" idea suggested by quantum physicists, but is this linguistic need the very source of the theory? The universe itself must bubble into existence and out of existence in order to have meaning, but must it not do so in some form of extra-universal framework. Let's be honest, that has stopped making sense to a finite mind trapped in a human body on the planet earth.

How, though, in the end, does any of this matter? It seems that the conclusion is hellish and suffering conditions are inevitable in this universe and all future universes. Additionally, it would seem that even if a master escapes a wheel, it is only this wheel, it will all have to be done again anyway in a bubbling multiverse. What's more (since there is only one thing), the *experience* of liberation from suffering is only that. It's an illusion or experience – no different than the illusion or experience of suffering claimed by so many others. Somehow this understanding seems like it has to be incomplete. Perhaps that's the wrong word; maybe irrelevant is more accurate? Is the conclusion that there is no way reason, thinking, or experience (mental, physical, or spiritual) can ameliorate our temporal condition? If so, is there any reason to avoid creating better and potentially *less accurate* religions. Why not the never ending "Right Hand of God" notion promised by Christianity or the

72 Virgins of Islam (or 72 raisons) or the ultimate triumph of Zoroastrian "good" over evil, or ... or... well, I'm not sure what one gets in johnism. I guess one should think of it as god's surprise and delight at what you've imagined. And while that's still an anthropomorphic concept, I can't help but think 'god' would be more excited about what was invented than what was already the case (and unknowable except through faith)?

—particularly if it was really great!

Maybe there are kinds of suffering similar to the mountains about which Donovan sings. The first, and unenlightened kind, is a terrible burden that crushes and dooms humanity. Second, however, mankind learns to overcome his normal, animal-creature state and holds his mind to his thusness. This at least seams sure, as noted in the legendary Cartesian stab at eschatology (Descartes' search for an irreducible or *a priori* starting point), one would seem to be undeniably having (at the very least) the illusion of experience. Though it might not have led to the excellent set of follow-on decisions Descartes had hoped for, it does remain a core of being. "I think therefore I am" and until we're prepared to come to grips with the idea that it's an accident we must deal with that fact. I am: Therefore I suffer (by extension).

Or, to quote Kurt Cobain, "Here we are now, entertain us: I feel stupid and contagious."

This leaves two interesting choices: A.) It's all a sad accident B.) Individual suffering is irrelevant (an idea that faith defangs somewhat). Choosing B allows one to align with the decision (inevitability?) to come back eternally, ignoring one's own illusions to help with those of others to no end. Or, at least to do so until someone comes up with a better way to imagine it, one that really amazes God!

...first there is terrible suffering, then there is no suffering, then there is!

CII

Though drink has rotted my high reputation,
Reject it I will not, while I yet breathe,
Wondering often what the vintners buy
Equal in value with the wine they sell.

CONVERSATIONAL COMMERCE OF LOST SOULS

There are few things as depressing as an ignored sports program playing out on a TV high in the corner of a bar at an upscale mostly business hotel – it is somehow the conversational commerce of lost souls.

Notre Dame is leading Syracuse and Colorado will play Oklahoma State later, what do you think will happen? We are surrounded by several tons of marble and tapestry playing out a delicate balance of faux opulence. The intent to create an illusion of luxury or specialty is undermined by the utilitarian function. I do love the fact that it is quiet and no one bothers me. I can read, watch the contest, or make small talk at my leisure.

Would you believe I am a mere 11.8 miles from home? My wife and I have fled our usual dwelling just long enough to create some semblance of vacation. I work at a pre-IPO technology company and she is assistant-directing a play that recently had great success in England. Normally, we would be out at a museum, movie, or shopping, but she experienced insomnia last night and I've just begged the front-desk personnel for an extension of our already generous 4pm check out. She finally fell asleep at 3pm and I could not bear to wake her, so I successfully pleaded for a 6pm checkout. Maybe they'd understood my plight, maybe more than I'd care to admit. Or maybe they thought we were heavy drug users...who knows?

She'd love these mixed nuts though. She loves to pick through things to find tasty morsels – nutty little bitch. On Valentine's Day, she leaned in seductively to whisper in my ear that she was a "*naughty little bitch*." Unfortunately, I heard, "nutty little bitch" and I looked shocked and exclaimed, "Why do you think that?" I was somewhat incredulous that she should really think something like that in those words and express it in that way. Mine was clearly not the desired reaction, though at this point I'm not sure what the 'right' response would have been. Perhaps I was meant to say, "You want to be naughty?" or "You want to show me?" but what with the naughty/nutty confusion it would seem I killed the moment.

I blame it on reality television. I hate it and I am certain it is the ultimate death of art and triumph of the banal. If one seeks proof of declining empire or culture – as in Rome – there can be no greater litmus test than the proliferation of reality programming (e.g. the coliseum). Being in the L.A. milieu, however, I am subject to the ignominy of coming up with my own reality TV idea.

I cannot claim to have done all of this damage myself; I actually created the idea with a friend who was doing sound design on a play I wrote. Yes, I further admit to having written a "play" – as if it were 1960 or I still lived in NY. Neither are the case, and there is no use for my play, but I merrily persist as though someone somewhere might want or need this bauble.

The thought of the brilliant and brave people who ventured forth to admire it makes this admission that much more painful. (Notre Dame is up 7 at the half, if anyone is more interested in that fact) So, out with it!

The idea is called *Home Sweet Homeless* and it certainly crosses some line somewhere, though I am convinced it would be successful as reality TV. Twelve homeless and certifiably psychologically-challenged people are placed in a luxurious home in the Hollywood Hills and forced to compete in a variety of tasks requiring social skills and teamwork. The last homeless person remaining, the only one not to have been voted back to homelessness, is given the house. Now, of course, the contestants are all given career guidance, as well as health, nutrition, and psychological counseling while they are in the home. But why is it so wrong? Could it be the fact that many will be voted back to a sub-par existence? That happens on *Survivor, Big Brother*, and *Fear Factor* every week. Maybe it's choosing the homeless or the mere idea of helping them for fun, profit, and entertainment? Maybe some things, like reality TV, are just wrong all the time.

L

This world must long survive our poor departure,
Persisting without name or note of us.
Before we came it never grudged our absence,
When we are gone how can it feel regret?

DATING

Oh strange. This life... Oh so very, very strange. I don't know how these thoughts get into my head. I was wondering, if I were to make an entry on a dating site like eHarmony or match.com, how it would go. I started amusing myself that I might write something like this to begin my, whatever you call it, profile...

If I'm Digger the Hermaphrodite you're:
1. A fingernail
2. A toenail
3. Lamisil
4. Not amused
5. Too attuned to our media-saturated surroundings to escape noticing an annoying, unfubsy, brand-icon-cum-scaremmercial (though you wish you weren't)
6. Convinced I've just insulted hermaphrodites everywhere
7. Convinced I've just insulted dermatophytes everywhere
8. Convinced I've got too much time on my hands or lack basic sanity
9. No longer reading this
10. Mildly amused

Then I stopped to really think about that. WHO WOULD ANSWER SUCH A POSTING? I always joke about being mad, weird, or almost completely stupid...but it's always seemed like a sort of joke. Suddenly I'm looking at this nonsense I've been thinking (above) and I realize that if I read that I'd probably shout "Freak!" and move on to the next picture of a potential date. To be honest, I'd probably only read the profiles of the images that appeared attractive and that mostly to screen out stupidity. Am I a hypocrite? A fraud? I think I've just concluded that I would not date me. And that's saying something because I've spent many years hoping I was somewhat of a catch. So either I'm a hypocrite, expecting someone else to see in me what I don't, or I'm shallow, or both.

"Shallow Hypocrite seeks spiritual, loving significant other that sees past material."

I wanted to make sure I spelled dermatophyte correctly, because I wasn't entirely sure of that – nor what the drug was called. "Lamisil," it turns out. So I started searching the internet and discovered this weird site that had some kind of tribute to "Digger" (the CGI creature Novartis uses to sell their product) and then all these quotes. I was sucked in. I couldn't stop reading the site. I had a realization that I probably suffer from not caring about anything. In some ways this is good; for example, I'm not a religious zealot because I believe in many paths to the same peak.

When you realize that people are very likely to think whatever they think despite your best efforts and arguments, and history's as well, you lose something. You gain something insofar as you attain a kind of peace (if it's not apathy), but you lose something that drives great writers. You also lose drive in general. You smile knowingly when you read:

"*Ambition is a poor excuse for not having sense enough to be lazy.*"
-- Edgar Bergen, via Charlie McCarthy

But, you then read:

"*Though we would like to live without regrets, and sometimes proudly insist that we have none, this is not really possible, if only because we are mortal. When more time stretches behind than stretches before one, some assessments, however reluctantly and incompletely, begin to be made. Between what one wishes to become and what one has become there is a momentous gap, which will now never be closed. And this gap seems to operate as one's final margin, one's last opportunity, for creation. And between the self as it*

is and the self as one sees it, there is also a distance even harder to gauge. Some of us are compelled, around the middle of our lives, to make a study of this baffling geography, less in the hope of conquering these distances than in the determination that the distance shall not become any greater."
-- James Baldwin

And you get a little scared. Why? Because you don't have that. You don't have that sense of there being some other better you that you should be or should have been. You are so completely pleased with yourself it's bordering on ridiculous. And "AYE THERE'S THE RUB" is it all just a sort of acceptance of the status quo in order not to suffer the pain of comparison to imagined greatness? Yet you know all greatness is just that "imagined." Or is it? Wherever you've applied yourself you've been good. You feel in the depth of your being that any kind of 'Happiness through Achievement' or 'Greatness through Achievement' is doomed to failure. Is Tom Brady inherently any happier than you? ...or either of you any more or less than Einstein, Gandhi, or John Doe?

There is just the doing of things, but then what things and why? Might it not be the greatest thing in the world and the greatest driving force in your creativity to be a Marxist, Communist, or somethingist? I am a professed *johnist*, but one of the central tenets of *johnism* (after salvation is personal) is that you can't DO anything to get it. YOU ARE IT> it is an ethos that inclines you rather to non-active transformation (there needs to be a word for this). Evolving through not-doing... what does that even mean? But how will any of this help? It excites you to read:

"*Not to censor is an act of moral will, a commitment. At some point early in his career a young writer must come to it, like a kind of the Hippocratic oath. If he can think something, he will say it; if it says itself, he will not strike it; if he can write it, he will publish it. The writing does not belong to 'himself.' The refusal of censorship and self-censorship is, of course, essential for the use of writing against lying and oppressive regimes; but it also makes a writer a thorn in the side of his own political cause: He gets nice about the slogans; he can't say the half-truth; he states the case of the opposition better than is convenient; and so forth....The spontaneity, the free origination, of writing is one aspect of a writer's disinterestedness; he does not will it, but he is present with it.*"
-- Paul Goodman, Speaking and Language: Defense of Poetry (1971)

And you think, "Yes there must be an absolute banishment of censorship," maybe even in all life. Then you think how impractical that would be, but in writing, surely, yes surely in writing you must do this... and as suddenly as you were moved to associate with this idea of eradicating censorship you feel alienated and inept at the thought that nothing you ever write or say would effect "lying and oppressive regimes." You will never be a thorn in the side of your own political causes because you have none. You recognize the need to fight deceitful and oppressive behavior in yourself, but in the body politic, you wonder how anyone would get by without it. You understand oppression and loath it, but all sides have been committing atrocities against all other sides for so long that it's impossible to maintain anything short of a government's own self-righteous end. You come to suspect Ken Wilber of being a "dangerous man." But still, you feel right. You think, yes possibly, but not probably, and then you read:

"*Regarding a certain fetishized conception of theory, E.P. Thompson wrote (a quarter century ago) that it "has now lodged itself in a particular social couche, the bourgeois lumpen-intelligentsia: aspirant intellectuals, whose amateurish intellectual preparation disarms them before manifest absurdities and elementary philosophical blunders, and whose innocence in intellectual practice leaves them paralyzed in the first web of scholastic argument which they encounter; and bourgeois, because while many of them would like to be 'revolutionaries,' they themselves are the products of a particular 'conjuncture' which has broken the*

circuits between intellectuality and practical experience (both in real political movements and in the actual segregation imposed by contemporary institutional structures), and hence they are able to perform imaginary revolutionary psycho-dramas (in which each outbids the other in adopting ferocious verbal postures) while in fact falling back upon a very old tradition of bourgeois elitism..."
-- The Poverty of Theory and Other Essays (Merlin, 1978).

And damnit, it just doesn't seem fair. And it is a bit creepy as this particular procession of thought seems to be aimed directly at the achilles heel of your belief system (or lack thereof). It is readily apparent that I could neither write such a thing nor probably even take it seriously, and yet that very fact dooms me to this couche-bourgeois-amateur-elitism that is paralyzed intellectually and physically in the face of something someone would call "practical" or "realistic." And still, you know you are not in the wrong, completely, yet. And as you wonder at the idea of "actual segregation imposed by contemporary institutional structures" you find your understanding hollow. Instead of feeling Ye-Olde-Wilberian pride at understanding where and why such things happen, you kind of wonder what it might be like to feel that, in fact, all these things were happening intentionally and that perhaps a thorough re-evaluation of contemporary society (as manifest in institution and probably rebellion) might just be the key.

Yes, that's it, *America 2.0,* and you can believe in such things being noble or worthy of pursuit in their own right, but you still can't believe it will make a difference. Because everything that you've ever known about human interaction you learned in kindergarten when the kids danced about you in a circle singing "John, John, the Leprechaun went to school with nothing on." And you know that nothing has changed since then. *America 2.0* won't make a difference because the status quo is what people want for the most part. And you have an advantage over this E.P. Thompson insofar as you see he just believes too powerfully in his own private Idaho (or *America 2.0*). Then you are given a salve for your burning head:

"*The truth is that most of my life is spent in tasks so utterly mundane and banal that it would require new developments in narrative theory simply to try to relate them.*"
-- Michael Bérubé

However, as salves work topically, your momentary surcease of anxiety is revealed to have been induced by a placebo. No, it is no help at all. Why did it feel good for a second to read it? Like stepping out of a sauna for a breath of fresh air, and it doesn't matter how cold it is for second, there is no cold too cold for at least a few breaths... then you're in Wyoming in January and you realize this just won't do. It was a palliative, nice, but useless. It was candy for the mind, but then you remember just how much you love candy for the mind and decide that there is some kind of merit to be reserved for it. It's not going to save the day, but it is delicious even if brief and illusory.

Wait, though, wait, wait, wait, wait -- it can't -- this page cannot go all the way there. Can it? Oh yes, it begs, read on:

"*But indeed Conviction, were it never so excellent, is worthless till it convert itself into Conduct. Nay properly conviction is not possible till then; inasmuch as all Speculation is by nature endless, formless, a vortex amid vortices: only by a felt indubitable certainty of Experience does it find any centre to revolve round, and so fashion itself into a system. Most true it is, as a wise man teaches us, that "Doubt of any sort cannot be removed except by Action." On which ground, too, let him who gropes painfully in darkness or uncertain light, and prays vehemently that the dawn may ripen into day, lay this other precept well to heart, which to me was of invaluable service: "DO THE DUTY WHICH LIES NEAREST THEE," which thou knowest to be a duty! Thy second duty will already have become*

clearer. . . .The Situation that has not its Duty, its Ideal, was never yet occupied by man. Yes here, in this poor, miserable, hampered, despicable Actual, wherein thou even now standest, here or nowhere is thy Ideal: work it out therefrom; and working, believe, live, be free. Fool! The Ideal is in thyself, the stuff thou art to shape that same Ideal out of: what matters whether such stuff be of this sort or that, so the Form thou give it be heroic, be poetic? O thou that pinest in the imprisonment of the Actual, and criest bitterly to the gods for a kingdom wherein to rule and create, know this of a truth: the thing thou seekest is already with thee, "here or nowhere," couldst thou only see! . . . . Be no longer a Chaos, but a World, or even Worldkin. Produce! Produce! Were it but the pitifullest infinitesimal fraction of a Product, produce it, in God's name! 'Tis the utmost thou hast in thee: out with it, then. Up, up! Whatsoever thy hand findeth to do, do it with thy whole might. Work while it is called Today; for the Night cometh, wherein no man can work."
-- Thomas Carlyle, Sartor Resartus

And there you are, forced to say, OK...not even sure to what, but OK...OK...OK, OK, OK! And if it must be that you write in circles and attack windmills and oppose the vicious-sympathetic-racist-childish-understandable-horrific-pseudo-institutional-murderous-greedy-young-and-completely-ordinary ill of our day, our America, our minds, hearts, souls...well then, I guess you must.

There it is; I've done it. I've found my daily rabbit-hole, my silly copout, my quixotic windmill. Is that what I do? Do I meander in a seeming ur-struggle with sense of self and creative power until discovering a witty pièce de résistance, then duck out the back door? Apparently so. How then can I ever care about anything enough to write with uncensored truth? Particularly as I am a reluctant epistemological solipsist who doesn't cotton much to the "T" word anyway. Maybe that's just it. For the reluctant epistemological solipsist (RES) there are only two states: Pooh with a potful of 'hunny' or Eeyore on his forgotten birthday. It will be one or the other incessantly, and this honeypot looks as half-empty as one can imagine.[8]

---

[8] Though the quotations are notably historical, the connection to pictures of Digger originated on a website run by Scott McLemee.

BLARG

(new word)

Blarg also **Blargger | Blargging** (v.): \'blȯrg, 'blärg\ Drunken, aggressively partisan, or otherwise irascible ranting by way of text posted on the Internet (or tweet sent to mobile phone). Similar to its cousin blogging, blargging is more quixotic and less rational. Though, it has been suggested that many of today's blogs are actually blargs. Contrary to popular belief, intoxication is not a prerequisite.

"Did you see Orly Taitz' latest blarg about joining forces with *Tea-Partier's for a Cleaner Gulf* to throw replicas of the Obama/Hope poster into the sea so that they might simultaneously express outrage and absorb oil?"

THE SYSTEM IS BROKEN

Part 2: Without

I had to fly to Denver. I was starting a new job so it was going to be a short trip. I parked in Lot C at LAX. My return flight landed around 11pm on a Sunday, I was anxious to get some sleep before an early day of work. I remembered where my car was... I was pretty sure. It was close to D8, I remembered by making it the word "date." If I could remember the word date, I could surely find my car when I got home. And, I assured myself, I can remember the word date. However, I could not find my car. I walked and walked and increasingly doubted my memory. I became upset at the silliness of using a word like date to remember where your car was and not writing down a number or taking a picture with your cell phone. Though, slowly, I began to have another thought. Someone stole my car. It was now after midnight, I gave up and went to find the parking lot office.

I told the gentleman working there what had happened and he pointed me to a phone where I could call the police. I did. After a bit of explaining on my part and searching on their part, they announced that they had my car. Why? I asked. "Because it had expired tags," they said. I sighed. I tried to explain that I had already paid and it was some kind of colossal screw up at the DMV. They didn't care. "Well, what" I asked, "do I have to pay to get it out."

"You have to have your registration first."

"Where can I get that?"

"At the DMV."

"But...they're closed."

"Yup."

"What do I do now?"

"Can't help you."

I hung up the phone. I couldn't believe this was happening. I thought for a minute. It was after 1AM and I didn't really want to call a friend to drive down to LAX at that time. Additionally, I would have to drive to the DMV on my lunch hour the next day, and then back to the airport to get my car assuming I could work it all out. I asked if there was a rental car company nearby. The parking lot office attendant said there was, and that I could walk. Nothing is close at the airport. It was nearing two in the morning when I arrived at the Alamo rental car desk. There was a line. It wasn't long, but still at 2AM? It would be just shy of $50 for a walk-up rental of a subcompact for one day. I didn't care; I was done, beat, couldn't think or move and I had just walked for over a half hour with a heavy bag. I wanted to go home. By the time I made it home and dug up all my cancelled checks and letters for the next day, it was around 4 am. I slept a few hours and went to work.

On my lunch hour, I went to the DMV. The lady at the desk said I didn't have my registration sticker because I still owed money. I told her that I'd paid everything including for a ticket that I didn't get and a late penalty on that ticket and a late penalty on my registration. She didn't believe me. I slapped cancelled checks on the counter, somewhat defiantly. She said I hadn't "Paid in full." I said, "Do the math. There are checks here totaling $519, which is way more than the registration, plus I've been up until 4 in the morning and had to pay for a rental car." She got out a calculator. She called over a manager. It wasn't, it turns out now that they couldn't plausibly accuse me of not having paid, that I hadn't paid, but that they needed proof of insurance. I sent that with my first payment, I told them. Well, they didn't have it now, and would have to have it again...

"Where's your proof of insurance?"

"It's in my car, which is impounded at LAX."

"Well, you'll have to go get it."

"They won't let me have my car until I bring them my registration, plus I have to work, plus I'm paying $50/day for this rental car, plus THIS IS ALL YOUR FAULT!"

"Sorry, we can't let you have your registration without proof of insurance."

"I've been on the same Allstate policy for seven years! Can't you just check the system? Call the airport impound yard? Call Allstate?"

"Sorry."

"I have a cell phone...here, I'll call Allstate!"

"Sir, you can't just call someone, I don't know who is on the other end of the phone."

"There must be something we can do?"

"You can call your agent and have them fax proof of insurance over."

"Thanks. Do you have a fax number?"

Thank god for the miracle of cell phones. I called my agent; they faxed over proof of insurance. The DMV gave me a sticker. I was hungry.

After work, I drove to the airport returned the rental car and walked to the airport police department. They wanted $185 which was something like $125 for towing and $12/day for storage. I explained, I showed cancelled checks, plus the registration sticker they had given me, this was all a big mistake. "Doesn't matter, you can't have your car back until you pay." The police officer was behind a thick glass window. We were speaking through a tiny slotted vent, he didn't care. He didn't even look at my cancelled checks. He knew his line, "You have to pay to have your car released." That was all he was ever going to say. Though, I'll give him some credit – the most credit anyone in this story gets – he did say he was sorry about my plight. I threw him a credit card. He wrote on forms and gave me receipts. He explained about the long walk to where the car was actually "stored." I started walking.

Now, you're thinking this story is over. You're thinking, if there is anything more to add that I'll be making it up. But, you would be wrong. If there is such a thing as karma (carma?), I must have offended the gods mightily, because this story is not over. But let's take a quick look at the math again: $45 for ticket I never got, $65 for late payment, $149 penalty for late registration, $50 for rental car, $185 for towing and storage = $494.00 I've given the DMV $799.00 in total of which $494.00 is due to their incompetence. Don't get me started about the countless trips to Kinkos, to the DMV instead of lunch, the hours writing letters and getting stamps, the waste of time or the loss of sleep. And...and...and... it's not over?

LXI

I shall possess myself of a great goblet
With pipes of wine for its replenishment,
Annulling former ties to Faith & Reason
By marriage with this daughter of the vine.

HAND-CRANKED

I'm a coffee person, and have thought for some time that knowing oneself is an essential component to whatever this "living" turns out to be. Thus, if it winds up that coffee is bad for you, I will be a person who does things (more things) that are bad for you. My quest for the accoutrement of the habit, today, led me to no fewer than 9 establishments in search of a simple grinder I could control. And, I guess in a retail-critique way, a dearth of help.

The first thing that becomes apparent is the tendency to find fancy machines that take pre-created creamer-like packages and force steam through them resulting in the "perfect" single cup. Is that really what we want these days? Are we really a society that is progressing towards some sort of Gilliam-esque[9] über-future of disposable perfection? One cup at a time?

I just want to have my hands on/in the elements: Grind (coarseness), water temperature, exposure to

---

[9] Terry Gilliam – Monty Python member and director of many surreal classics such as *Brazil, Time Bandits, Baron Munchausen, and The Fisher King.*

the coffee (time steeped)…stuff like that. To that end, though I'm not sure I can afford the machines that allow me to manipulate the exposure to and temperature of the steam, I'm fairly certain I want to control the grind. For as long as I can remember, and probably somewhere lost in a box, I've had a faceless, white, bean-crusher that would spin when you pressed the top and do a good job of smashing things up inside (pulverizing). I can only admit that I've finally come to terms with having taken it for granted. Alas.

This world doesn't want you to crush your own beans, or so it would seem. My quest starts (can we really call it a quest; will I always give in to my penchant for melodrama?) at CVS, because it happens to be close and convenient and "You never know what they have." Indeed, this one has a coffee section and even a grinder. There is a kind of coffee machine there for $9.99, which would remain the cheapest thing of any sort that occurred on the entirety of the journey. I think a latte at Starbucks is $3.95 plus tax itself. So, I'm almost tempted to buy this just to see what's going on with it. They do have one grinder. It's approximately $25 for what looks to be a simple spinner by something like CoffeeMate? I don't know; next to the $9.95 maker it suddenly seems a bit pricey for CVS, but I may wind up going back to it.

Coffee Stores:
By now, I need coffee just to look for coffee and go to a Starbucks that happens to be next door. They have some gift-oriented "supply" or "accoutrement" focused stuff on a shelf just in case (and probably for decoration). There is a French-press there that catches my interest. I ask the woman working the counter for a triple-shot-latte and how much for the French-press? She doesn't know (she says). I'm wondering who does? We seem to be at an impasse? I can't really acquire the product for an imaginary sum and she seems to have no intention of finding out if she or anyone else in the store will ever come close to having an "idea" about how much such a thing might be. Should I just take it? She's looking at the next person in line. I decide it's not worth finding out. So—no French-press from this Starbucks and no grinders.

I get the opportunity to peruse both a Tully's and a Peet's along the path of this "search". The counter-person at Tully's provides directions to a Williams-Sonoma and some form of blandishment regarding their exchange program. The intention is nice. Tulley's has some French-press options, but all in the $30 (one cup) to $50 range, which comes across as excessive and "gifty". The staff at Peet's is too busy to interact and does not have anything in the grinder-world at which to look.

Kitchen Supply:
Cost Plus World Market—I don't know if they have a coffee section, but (as an aside) they generally have a great wine selection and it holds true in this case. They also offer a small coffee-enthusiasm oriented spot that features a unique machine with a dedicated grinder ($80). However, it doesn't offer much in the way of features apart from the ability to store many days of whole beans in a rubber-topped tub (dubious, I suspect, as a requirement). They have a couple of offerings in the French-press category, but nothing really worth noting and in the upper $20s to $40s. All in all, more noteworthy for their wine offerings... but that's not saying nothing (double-negatives are).

Crate & Barrel—they have only one grinder offering, but feature an array of seemingly "special" $400 makers that utilize the aforementioned pre-packaged, half-n-half looking, plastic cupule of potential coffee-perfection. I believe Gevalia will give you something mail-order for free along with a year-long subscription to their bean service. That is not to imply that these makers aren't better than such an idea, nor that they aren't good in their own right, but don't we want to be a part of this "making"? Isn't making coffee a lot like life?

Sur Le Table—this is a very nice store in my mind (conceptually that is) and probably has a great deal of price-worthy kitchen and tableware. Their coffee area features more in terms of grinders and French-presses than Crate & Barrel, but is that saying anything worth repeating? They have a worktable dedicated to the exploration of steaming ground beans into "coffee", but it is functioning more as a display—not staffed to make the argument for the automatic per-cup perfection machines that seem to be their raison d'etre qua coffee.

I stop by a place called Teavana also, but they (hardly surprising in this weather) have only Tea and steeping tricks-of-the-trade.

Finally, I arrive at the Williams-Sonoma to which the Tully's employee had referred in the beginning. They actually have a hand-grinder in stock in addition to a few French-presses. At this point, I only take the hand-grinder. I experience the manufacturing by "Hario" to be at least a little daunting. One must hand-screw the central mechanism-grind stone to secure the "coarseness" setting and then, of course, hand-crank the apparatus. Though it is an indeterminate amount of work at this point, I have to confess that I'm excited to do it. It's not an accident that I get to participate in my own coffee making. I only hope that the metaphor for life applies to everyone. I suppose "I hope" that everyone *wants* this to be the case. I also hope that I continue to enjoy hand-cranking some beans into (an albeit brief) existence as a way of thinking about/participating in the joy of... steeping, grinding, brewing, ..."creating"?

This is really it. Take your time to make whatever it is you imagine making. That's what it's about.

LXII

As one familiar with all exoterics
Of being and not being, who has plumbed
The abyss of shame, how can I greet as valid
Any condition short of drunkenness?

NEO-BUDDHISM

(PPP: Poorly Paraphrased Parables)

A pilgrim was journeying to see the Buddha and he ventured past another man practicing dreadful asceticism. This ascetic was standing on one foot, bald-headed and naked in the burning sun, atop an anthill. His pealing and red flesh crawled with ants and yet he maintained a quiet dignity and addressed the traveler as he passed. "Excuse me sir, could I inquire where you're going?" he asked. The traveler replied, "I seek an audience with the Buddha." The man on the ant hill furthered, "If you find him, would you ask him how many more lifetimes I must lead before I achieve liberation from the wheel of samsara?" The traveler indicated that he would and continued his journey.

Later, the pilgrim passed a wildly drunken man. He was drinking from a gourd and furnished with a broad leaf containing all manner of delicacies. While singing his heart out, he would on occasion scream then roar with laughter. He made very little sense from afar, but when the pilgrim came near enough he stopped his revelry and shouted for the traveler to join him. The traveler replied that he was seeking an audience with the Buddha, and he did not wish to interrupt his journey. The drunken man cried out, "If you find him, would you ask him how many more lifetimes I must lead before I achieve liberation from the wheel of samsara?" The traveler said that he would and pressed on with his journey.

(apparently it's a very popular question)

The pilgrim journeyed for months, but eventually succeeded in his quest for an audience with the Buddha. One day, he found himself walking along the same road he had previously traveled. He was surprised to see the ascetic in the same place on the road and holding the same position as he had before, though perhaps more worn by the piteous suffering to which he was subjecting his body. The ascetic recognized him immediately despite his physical distress. "Friend," he called, "were you successful in finding the Buddha?" The pilgrim replied that he had been. "And were you able to ask my question of him?" The traveler said that he had and added, "The Buddha's words for you were that you had three more lifetimes before you will achieve what you seek." At that, the man let out a horrendous moan that chilled the very air and nearly knocked him from his one-legged perch.

The traveler left him weeping, but continued on his way. Quite surprisingly, in the same place further along the road where he had previously encountered the drunken man singing and eating, what should he spot other than the same man engaged in yet another revelry of nearly identical farce. He was quite beside himself, but as the traveler approached he too recognized this passerby from months ago. "Tell me," he shouted, "how did you fare in your quest to gain an audience with the Buddha?" The traveler responded that he had indeed seen the Buddha. "And did you ask him my question?" said the drunken man. "I did" replied the traveler. "Annnnddd" sang or slurred the gourd-guzzling singer? The traveler pointed across a nearby field and began, "Do you see that oak tree over there? The really big one—the one the size of a barn and covered with leaves?" The crazed singer strained his gaze, but there was only one truly and magnificently large oak tree to which the traveler must be referring. "Why yes, of course..." he warbled. "The Buddha says you have more lives to live than there are leaves on that tree." To this day one can hear the echoes of the hardy "Hooooooray!" the man whooped before returning to his incoherent crooning.

XLVII

Dear Love, when you are free to slough your skin
And become naked spirit, soaring far
Across God's Empyrean, you will blush
That you lay cramped so long in body's gaol.

START

two people confront each other in the night
a deserted and lightless street—an alley
out of the way—nowhere
one pulls out a knife
he says, "Give me all your money!"
the other pulls out a gun, and says
"Drop your shit and get out of here."
the first inches closer, pressing his knife
"I'm not kidding!"
the second squints his determination,
"Neither am I"
they are very close, there is a struggle
the gun barks, flesh rips, blood splashes
one figure collapses to the ground, the other flees the alley
we don't know what to say about such an event
some say, "Well, one less mugger in the world" – cheerfully
but it is still sad
yet others say, "That's just how it's done."

C

So lovingly I drink, the wine's bouquet
Will scent the air where I lie underground;
A topper treading past my grave will pause
To sniff, and find himself ignobly drunk.

WHAT'S WRONG WITH YOU?

Part One: Everything Is Storytelling
I'll begin this story with another story. This introduction is about a girl I used to date who had a penchant for beginning conversations, "You know what's wrong with you?" Whether or not she was correct in noting some of the myriad problems I possessed and that she had observed, there was definitely a conversation working into our dialogue and the nature of that ongoing story was exactly what, at any given time, may or may not be wrong with me.

I believe that everything we encounter in life embodies a degree of storytelling, ranging from actual stories (such as film/tv) to cars, couches, computers and remote controls. We utilize these stories in meeting people, building bridges, seducing coeds, or selling automobiles. Even forks are telling stories if we tune into them (pun intended). Perhaps there's a great business book to be written helping enterprises get in touch with their vision statements[10]. Why we do what we do, is as important as what we do. But, back to the driving story, one day I was trying to explain to my friend that we were developing a "*What's wrong with you*" dialogue or narrative to *our* 'story'. Without skipping a beat, she said, "You see, that's what's wrong with you." I did a spit take with my drink. Some things are just innate! I laughed.

Part Two: Putting The Cart Before The Horse
There was a time when the "audience" for entertainment was more focused. To put it in a village context, the shaman, medicine man, leader, or warriors would tell tales about their experiences of the world around the campfire. These were educated people telling stories that lived in a backdrop of a people's tradition. Even the early days of tv and radio purported to provide expertise and knowledge on the subjects they discussed. As our modes of communication and digital recording / sharing / broadcasting become more ubiquitous, the level of expertise naturally falls. This should not be a bad thing, but we must keep an eye out for the why and wherefore and what's right and what we should

---

[10] The CEO, director of marketing, product/project designers, and cleaning staff ALL benefit from a clearly defined and incorporated vision statement.

value. We face two tyrannies: The Majority and The Money. Let's refresh our use of the term Ochlocracy[11] –Majority Rule gone bad.

Alexis de Tocqueville[12] painted an image of the dangers a fledgling democracy might face, and it's not too far a stretch to apply these concerns to modern entertainment. We are losing degrees of discernment in our rush to share our piece of the opinion pie. There is no reason to single out Justin Bieber as there are many examples of "popularism" in the world. However, there is no argument that he "sells." Whatever it is he's doing, well or otherwise, there are people who want to pay to see it. "They vote with their dollars" is a common expression these days. The point here is not to critique the artist himself, but to question the steps that lead the public to these ochlocratic decisions.

There seems to be a growing desire to have a president we want to drink a beer with and not one that was influential at Harvard. We say that anything that makes money must be good – or, at the very least, it has THAT unassailable quality (in the face of

---

[11] An Ochlocracy is a system of Mass- or Mob-rule, typically implying the subversion of rights to majority opinion.
[12] A French political writer 1805-1859, best known for *Democracy in America*.

other nebulous qualities often lumped together in something we call discernment). Our society wishes to eradicate the pittance spent on PBS (due to the suffering economy), while electing those that can "afford" to run, and allowing unlimited corporate and Super-PAC contributions. Corporations don't need the status of "individuals" qua voting, they are composed precisely of individuals whose rights are already ensured. Also, money is not free speech, in fact, a plethora of money in any political context makes the decision like trying to listen to a conversation between a stadium-sized bullhorn and a cell phone with a surgical mask in a hole covered with a pillow. For speech to be free, both sides must be able to be heard.

To return to the cart-before-the-horse analogy, one imagines cartloads of Justin Bieber life-size cutouts beginning to drag the entire contraption downhill. I suppose it will all come to rest in some sort of geographical nadir (death valley?). So, what ought one do with/in our newly discovered digital-opinion oriented culture? Be the discernment you want to see?

Part III – Bad Metaphors & Balance

With the understanding of hindsight, I might have suggested that my friend (from part one) either couple her observations with something I do that she can tolerate, or even to phrase the entire question from the POV of what was good and what might be improved. This is mere semantics, but a constantly evolving and growing self-concept about how I'm getting better and better at more things each day is superior to a piece of baggage, a cart, or trailer in which I drag around my ever-expanding list of things "wrong with me."

Politics has put re-electability and money suffused lobbies first. They've combined two dangerous forces in illustrating that the money can deliver the majority in most cases. Rather than focus on what's right or what law leads to better society or which arguments make the most sense, there is a combination money/majority pulling most of the cart downhill. Can we make up descriptors like Ochlo-Oligarchical-Plutocracy (OOP)? Try saying that to someone and keeping a straight face. One might, but it's unlikely to change politics or entertainment. Unless we can hope for self-education to go hand-in-hand with freedom, we will be saying *OOP* in a more permanent fashion. In order to utilize educational opportunities, we need to provide them. That's why a politics of defunding NEA/PBS, with costs below 1% of the budget, makes so little sense. Don't think of it as funding art you don't like, think of it as making available education you can't get without putting a cart full of popularity in front of a team of horses and watching them get pulled into the ditch. Think of educated alternatives not so much as *what's wrong with oneself*-society but more an inspiring way to improve one's... je ne sais quoi.

XLII

Raise the bowl high, like tulip-cups at Nauroz,
And if the moon-faced one has time to spare
Drink gloriously deep, for brutal Time
Will strike you down with never a warning yell.

WHO ME?

What does it mean... sorry, I plan to discuss this later, but I was just having this thought and wanted to write it down before I forget. Yes, that happens to me more frequently these days. Why? I guess we'll call it age. Have you ever, wow, am I segueing, have you ever thought of life as a series of experiences you didn't see coming (who does) and therefore apply the term "age" or "aging" to the experience? Because what else would you call it? The very concept of time passing or accruing in an identity (sense of self or singularity) is what enables the thought - experience in the first place.

You'll think I'm joking, but even in typing that first paragraph, in which I began to express another thought (above), I very nearly forgot the whole purpose of what I purported to be planning to discuss later. Really? I might be losing my mind. I know I have questions that I think I want to go over, but I also feel the need to jot down a reminder in case I forget or no one is available. Wow!

So, the question I was / will be planning to bring up: What does it mean if you ... oh dear is this becoming ironic... I just realized I'm writing down this question... sorry and digressing mid-segue, so... what does it mean if you find yourself thinking that you don't want to write something? In this case, it's a completely benign... I was going to say, but this belies the question... I also seem hooked on ellipses (apparently) and digressions...so point: What does it mean if you find yourself thinking you don't want to write something, but you want say it instead? Have you had this thought? Does it mean you've caught a whiff of your own subconscious, or that you really might suspect that you think something that you're not dealing with or recognizing fully or... and somehow writing it down cements something – an opinion? I can't say this is the thought or was the thought or I guess it's hard to express because there isn't a straight up "thought". An actual thought, I suspect, one would recognize or know. In fact, now that I am writing this, I am becoming aware of two sort of proto-thoughts... one is that I noticed about myself, somewhat as if I was a third person, this vague compulsion not to want to write something down: equivocating with myself?

The second, and follow on, and probably only now that I'm writing this, is that I'm writing you... or that "you" are the person with whom I wanted to discuss it, which must make you my subconscious in some fashion. That's true and not shocking and ... whatever, that it's you I'd want to talk to about something going on in life is not at all surprising, but in regard to this question the fact that it's you is also revealing... like catching myself not wanting to write something down.

Well I'm rambling, probably ... an odd combination of lack of sleep and mental instability, but for the first time (maybe new modes of communication throw themselves into the mix), suffice to say, I found myself 'near-thinking' or displaying an unformed aversion to using a mode of communication. I found the experience either unnerving or at least unfamiliar. I decided to ask you about it when I got a chance, realized that would be later, and then began to think I'd forget, and now am writing this down, which has become long, in order that I don't forget what I want to discuss.

I feel ridiculous.

XXXVI

Greedily to the bowl my lips I pressed
And asked how I might sue for green old age
Pressing its lips to mine, it muttered darkly
"Drink Up! Once gone you shall return no more!"

A HIDEOUS WORK OF PRETERNATURAL SUBJECTIVITY

At 8pm (7:58pm PDT to be precise) he looked up the words propitiate[13] and irenic[14] in the dictionary. The first, merely to confirm his suspicions: The second, to fill a void in his otherwise adequate vocabulary. Nothing, absolutely nothing, about this was interesting. To be completely honest, he didn't really do these things at this time. He wrote about doing them. This was perhaps interesting, but certainly the only telling thing he could, or probably ever would, reveal. With that, his vain and preposterous story, itself a rearrangement of countless vain and preposterous stories before it, was over ere it had begun.

The author may thus get around to saying that which, as noted *ubi supra*, has already been said in so many other ways by so many other writers – some of which

---

[13] Propitiate: To make propitiation or atonement; appease – or make peace.
[14] Irenic: Promoting or fitted to promote peace; pacific – non-confrontational.

are appreciably more talented. To say there is nothing new under the sun is merely to cloak the conundrum in aphorism. On the other hand, to say, "Ya gotta git up pretty early in th'mornin to fool grandpa" is to cloak the conundrum in colloquialism, which is a lot more fun to say. Say it ten times fast... trust me. *Cloak the conundrum in colloquialism... Cloak the conun...*

The effort to understand one's presence, not merely on this planet, but in general—that is to say, ones being (or 'dasein' as Heideggar would have it)—is probably the ultimate MacGuffin. Therefore, for *this* to be a hideous work of preternatural subjectivity, it will be essential to pursue said MacGuffin *ala Moby Dick* to the exclusion of any and all other thought. Having said that, it would seem an appropriate point at which to expound upon the titular intent. The title is, for reasons that cannot be elaborated upon at this juncture, a bit misleading. The intent is not merely to write "A Hideous Work..." but, more to the point, *the* most hideous work of preternatural subjectivity ever imagined. I dare say, dear reader, you must find yourself hard pressed to think it is off to anything short of an astonishing start.

The question of what to do, and here not so much the overly moral "What ought one do," but rather the more mundane, "What to do, I'm bored", enjoys a precarious chicken-and-egg relationship with one's existential or metaphysical grounding. Should we seek the soothing salve of solipsism, we should find there is naught to it but the recording, endlessly, of every thought and experience that deigns to dance across the stage of one's consciousness. And yet, what could seem more wretchedly sisyphean than to become this interminable "couch-potato" out of time watching oneself watch TV? Ganesha wept at the thought of billions and billions of selves watching themselves watch TV and he with a remote control, gripped tusk-like, whirling in each of his four arms in each of his thousand names still unable to turn them off.

Teleology! That is what we chiefly need, or at the very least a TV show that pretends to it. Alas, there can be no point to this tautological train other than to arrive back at the station. Toot! Toot! All aboard for TV land! What then, having conceded the high ground to Nickelodeon, is there to say for this sad story, this sad-happy story of a person, a narrator, doomed to a state wherein the only liberation was to tell an original story using pieces of other stories whose logical permutations had been surpassed exponentially long ago? Was it...was it simply to allow this profoundly, desperately, reductive state to wound him more than it had any other sentient being, to rain tears like the Mother of ALL BOMBS, to plunge straight through hades, purgatory, hell, black holes, and dark matter, to suffer the absolute and unspeakable, nay unimaginable? And then, and only then, to softly laugh at one's ingenious stupidity—to laugh and laugh until the thunder of one's laughter causes Bacchus to wet himself, Zeus to cower under the bed, and the singular one-and-holy trinity to put up the storm shutters and brace? Well now, that sounds just hideous enough to be true.

If you're Kemal Atatürk[15] *and you know it, clap your hands. If you're Kemal Atatürk and you know it, clap your hands. If you're Kemal Atatürk and you know it, then your state will surely show it; if you're Kemal Atatürk and you know it, clap your hands!*

---

15 Kemal Atatürk (1881-1938) President and founder of modern (secular) Turkey.

XXIII

Rise up, why mourn this transient world of men?
Pass your whole life in gratitude and joy.
Had humankind been freed from womb and tomb,
When would your turn have come to live and love?

THE AWARD

A man is walking home absent-mindedly. Everything seems very familiar to him: the humidity, the click-scratch of his steps, the colors and shapes of houses, and the soft rush of his breathing. Suddenly it all begins to fade and run together, and he finds himself looking over an enormous assembly from behind a podium. It is an awards ceremony of a size and grandiosity he has never imagined. Everyone is immaculately dressed sitting around tables looking very important. The tables are laden with the most exciting and intriguing foods, drinks, and decorations. Everything is shimmering in the bright gold light of spectacle and celebration. The man gapes at the shear impact and importance of the whole situation.

With an unsettling abruptness the entire crowd rises and applauds, and as the shock gives way to realization the man understands. He is the winner, he has been chosen, he is being honored with the highest award. Despite all the confusion the man feels he has done something to deserve the award; somehow it all seems right to him. He chokes his voice free in order to thank everyone. He is still unsure of exactly why he is being honored, but he feels all the struggle of his life paying off. The emotion overwhelms him; how can he ever thank them for realizing everything he has done? He begins trying to think of everyone he needs to thank, but intense feelings of joy and understanding tear his mind away as he approaches the cluster of microphones and is hailed with a galaxy of camera flash. He clears his throat to test the microphone and the room falls silent with expectation. "Thank-you", he blurts, "I guess everyone has a....a moment....and uhm.... I'm having one now." He pauses to regain control of his thoughts, which are racing beyond his ability to recognize them. He says, "I'd like to thank my mother and father for believing in me, and my...", he thinks of his best friend from childhood not being able to see his great moment. "...and my friend Chris, I wish he could see me today." He starts crying. "I love you!" he shouts into the air hoping his friend's spirit might somehow hear him. He realizes he is crying "I love you" in front of a crowd and returning his attention to them says, "I love you all! Thanks! And goodnight!"

As the man is walking off the stage, the crowd, sympathetically reveling in the man's emotion and the glory of his outburst and the whole evening, roars with its own cacophony of emotion. The man is thinking, "It has all finally come together", when suddenly he is walking home again as if someone had flipped a light switch shutting off an entire world.

The man looks around not immediately recognizing anything. Then he realizes he is somewhere near his home and that he had been on his way there. He wipes tears from his eyes and wonders if he has just been given an award or not. Several questions tug at his reason and sanity. If he was given an award who gave it to him, and why, and where are they now? If he was not given an award, should he be embarrassed for accepting it and feeling as if he had deserved such a thing?

WIKIMAUNDER

(new word)

Wikimaunder also **Wikimaundered | Wikimaundering** (v.): \'wi-kē-mȯn-dər\ Digressing from link to link to link on Wikipedia trying to come to a resolute state of understanding anything completely. In an attempt to brush up ones understanding of a word such as marxism, one winds up reading for three days, linking to myriad influential and tangential ideas ranging from neo-hegelianism to constructivist epistemology to deontological ethics.

"I'm sorry I'm late, but I wikimaundered from Britney Spears to supervenience and before I knew it, it was tomorrow."

THE SYSTEM IS BROKEN

Part 3: Me

On February 6th, on my way to work, almost an entire year since paying the original ticket, I was hit by a woman trying to make a left turn across bumper-to-bumper traffic on Olympic. It was morning and there are three lanes between 6AM and 9AM. Apparently she hadn't accounted for that or didn't see me. My car was to go into the shop for the next 6 weeks. About midway through that time, I received a note on my door saying I had a certified letter at the post office that I would have to sign for in person. This is a problem for me, as I work in Santa Monica and am not in the area I live between 8am and 6pm on most days, and the post office is only open from 9-5. I eventually made an effort to arrange to come into work late on March 16th, and I collected my letter. It was from the DMV and it was to inform me that, as I hadn't deigned to pay them for my towing and storage at LAX, they were putting a lien on my car and it would be sold at auction unless I paid them (with added penalties). Alternatively, I could respond to their letter announcing my disputation of these facts (which would serve to put the sale on another timeline) within 10 days. I thought to myself, 10 days from March 6th...hmm, that's today! Guess who is spending another lunch hour at the DMV?

It is at this point, that I must confess I was beginning to lose my mind. I couldn't bear the thought of yet another lunch hour at the DMV, more penalties, or really anything else to do with a ticket that I never got. I arrived at the DMV and produced the letter and asked what I should do about it. I posed this question, "How, if I had not paid the towing and storage fee, could I possibly have my car? Because we both know, they would never, ever, ever, ever, even if I was stuck at the airport at 2am with no way home, give me my car unless I paid the fee. Even, if that fee was imposed due to their personal error!"

"Well then," the lady behind the desk at the DMV said, "prove that you have the car."

"What?"

What? Indeed...I sighed, though it started to sound more like the moan of a wounded animal. "My car is at Paulee Auto Body. I have a rental car right now." Her solution, you ask? I should drive to Paulee Auto Body and get a police officer and have him fill out a form known as a Vehicle Verification Form and then expedite that form and my response to the address on the letter. I said, "You can't just keep doing this! I've paid this. I have my car. It was 15-minutes of meter time over a year ago! How do I make it stop? Is it ever going to end? Can't you just call them and tell them they've made a mistake?"

"Sir, calm down."

"The system is broken! There is a problem here, and nothing I do makes any difference. I can't drive on my lunch hour, which I've already spent here, out to the auto body shop and find an officer and have him fill out a form and get this in the mail to whomever by today. Can't you just enter something into the system that says I've been here and this is all your mistake!"

"Sir, the only mistake is that you done got your car impounded!"*

**This is the moment, when I developed an entirely new understanding for those unfortunate souls in our society that have "gone postal." I don't say that lightly. And, of course, I grieve for the innocent victims and their families. It isn't right, and it isn't funny. I've lost a brother, I know. But the system is broken, and sometimes it pushes you right up to the threshold of your capacity to take it anymore. This should never* *lead to violence, but I'd be lying if I said there was anything less than a sincere desire to jump across the counter and illustrate my point with my fist. I sighed, something in me died. I believe there must be some good men and women working for the DMV, but the person looking at me was not one of them.*

I growled, "How the HELL is it my mistake when I never got a !@$#@#$ ticket!" It was clear to her that we weren't going to have any further civil conversation. "I'll get a manager," she said, "Go to window 22."

"Breathe," I said to myself. When the manager came to window 22, I prefaced, "Listen, I'm sorry, I know none of this is your direct doing. But can you, just for a second, try to understand what's happening to me? I've paid over $500 now, for a ticket that I never got! I've had my car impounded at the airport, I've written god knows how many letters, it just won't go away. And you know, YOU KNOW, they would never give me my car at the airport if I hadn't paid them."

"Yes, sir, I'm sorry. There is nothing I can do. You have to get this form filled out and then send it in."

"Will that matter? Will they take it off of their lien sale list, and stop negatively impacting my credit score and not keep doing the same thing over and over?"

"Yes, sir. I mean, I can't promise you, but we'll try to take care of it."

"So, I can just ask any officer on the street?"

"Yes, and here is the form."

"Are you going to do anything to find out how this happened? I mean, isn't it odd that I paid this with a credit card and somehow your system wanted to put a lien on my car and sell it at auction? Do you report this? Flag it? Call the police impound yard at LAX and tell them there is something wrong?"

"No, that would be impossible."

Impossible...hmm, what a word? That's what everything to do with CLADPE and the DMV felt like to me, IMPOSSIBLE! I went back to work. I had given up on the impossible idea of getting an officer to go to the auto body shop, and filling out a form, and getting it postmarked or to the DMV that day (before they closed), and having any of those steps make a difference. It didn't matter what I did, it was all impossible. Besides, it was already 3pm on Friday,

March 16th and I had been on my lunch hour for more than an hour. I had lots of work to do at the office, and if I lost my job over this…well, wouldn't that be the icing on the cake.

Saturday I received a call from the auto body shop, I could pick up my car on Monday. Guess where I'd be Monday at lunch? Yep, they should install a salad bar. I drove to the DMV, waited in line, they said I had to pull my car over into a special inspection area. After waiting there about 15 minutes, it took the gentleman another 15 minutes to fill out the Vehicle Verification Form. He basically wrote down details describing my car, VIN #, license plate, color, # of doors, etc. Then he said, guess what? I could go wait in line again. I took a number, waited, proved that I was insured, proved that my vehicle was in fact in my possession with the form I had just received (which the lady at the counter took and attached to another form and set aside). "So they'll remove the lien and not sell my car at auction?" I asked.

"Yes, she said, once they get this form."

"And there is nothing else I have to do?"

"Nope."

She seemed almost cheery, I felt cheery but wary. I took my new sticker out and put it on the back of my newly repaired car. I was registered. With any luck, I wouldn't have to visit the DMV until March of the next year...with any luck... assuming the form finds its way to the right... I started to tense up thinking about people showing up for my car saying they had recently bought it at auction from the airport impound lot for the $185.00 those employees thought was still owed. Over five hundred dollars – not putting a price on gas, stamps, printing at Kinkos, or most importantly the hours and hours and hours of my life – and I'll never really be free from the thought that somehow, somewhere, some incompetence on the part of the system and those that operate it, will result in a new letter, about the same ticket, that no one can do anything about, because it didn't happen, because it's past 60 days, because there's nothing I can do, because change would be... impossible.

I sighed. I drove back to work.

XLIV

Khayaam, should you be drink with love, rejoice!
Or bedded with your heart's delight, rejoice!
Your end is no more than the whole world's end
Fancy yourself no longer there; then smile.

CIRCUMLOCUTION

aka
woody & sigmund
I think (poorly) therefore I am (poorly)
go dig a ditch

It is a very strange thing for something that conceives of itself (oneself) as temporal and limited (or at the very least its language) to try to say, write, or think something permanent or even infinite and certainly eschatological. What does it mean for a being that cannot experience or think these things to have a word encapsulating them? Eschatology – or the study of that which is posthumous, whether it be your own end or the end of "humanity" or the end of "the world" or "being" or the universe, does not make much sense to talk about and yet we do. We have concepts like infinity that we say and use and "mean something" to us, though realistically they are impossible thoughts for a brain. Therefore this condition, and I like to call it that more so than a thought process or a science (like eschatology), should most likely be thought of as a "way" (Tao) or "being". Any discussion of it is almost certain to be replete with quotation marks, italics, parenthesis, and all manner of other tools to imply "***meaning***" through the written word (more so even than because I like them).

So, this begins by presenting some notes I made while sitting in a coffee shop and finding that my thinking strayed either to self-referential circumlocution or to infinitely vague generalities (such that they lacked meaning by reflecting millions of opinions). It seemed to me at the time that I was unable to properly "think" any longer about any subject without what felt like an endless string of defining presumptions with assumed terms or simply redefined sub-definitions until everything was essentially reduced to "*Because that's how thinking works.*" We put our eyes "in" or "to" the playdoh[16] and it reflects what we say we see. EVERYTHING comes down to "This is where you are standing / looking" and that's what it looks like "to you" or "from there". Thus are reflected terms such as "no one is wrong" or "nothing is but thinking makes it so." I've said it before, "IF a person sees a little blue man, he or

[16] The "Playdoh" or playdough is a reference to the 'epistemological-solipsist' (me) view that nothing has reality or meaning worth discussing until it is beheld (or imagined). It refers to a sort of protoplasm waiting to congeal into meaning when painted or "played" by the senses, thus it is a "something there" to the materialists while perhaps irksome to subjective idealists.

she does." There is no point in saying that the person "doesn't" see it. You might say, at best, "They are lying." All of the rest of life is coming up with ways to influence, manipulate, convince, cajole, threaten, or otherwise "get" others to see life the way we do (in other words, to be right). Not everyone can be AS right, as Ken Wilber points out, but everyone who is telling their truth is at least somewhat so. Even those who are lying in order to get something are somewhat right, again, in their attempt at getting someone to respond to what they perceive to benefit them - i.e. they've decided the action is "right" in order to produce the result they desire (and lying is their tool).

At that, let me say no more about what all this is, for I shall surely fail. But let me instead write down the thought process at coffee, which had the effect of rendering my experience of thinking "useless." Some of it might be repetitive, as I've tried to condense the thought above, but it is also not easily laid out. Sometimes the train of thought is simply helpful.

Killing time in Boulder: I just bought a small bamboo booklet in order to write down my painful thesis, which is not "painful" because it is really releasing inner-nature. So what do I mean by painful: Difficult? Regrettable? Maybe it is a bit scary because in many ways it obviates what one does – or elevates it to a useless degree of importance. The thought is that ultimately all thought and action is circuitous, self-referential, yin-n-yang, infinitely expandable or otherwise contradictory. The $64K question is, is it therefore meaningless? Multiple meanings – yes – more than grains of sand on the beach? Yes. But, "-less" I don't know. What does it do to one's thought to say that nothing is absolute? What does it mean to say you hold in your mind the word "infinite"? What does it mean for a finite/temporal creature (if it is) to say or think "infinite"? We probably cannot really hold the thought. It's just the opposite or negation of finite (which is, in itself, a somewhat imaginary creation based on our size or perspective).

What does it mean to plumb the depths or "expanse" of the power or efficacy of your thinking? Is *flawed* or *faulty* merely insufficient? Your world "is" your weltanschauung "is". What does it *mean* to say we can't know what things *mean*? "I" sit here and drink coffee and write "I". I went to Seth's birthday. I go to Marci-Faye's and see Lucy, etc. But if "I" don't feel "I" do it, then "I" just put these damned quotation marks around my life. What's the point? The thought, just like the writing, etc. is futile. The woman near me just said, "That's my son." – Now that is as concrete as it gets. I simply fail to be if being is merely doing, or I do little / mean little. Is this why Hunter S. drank, drugged, gambled, and ultimately pulled the plug? Thinking was over? Pointless? Doomed?

Doing? Failing? Interesting? Right? I want to put quotes around everything. Is that ultimately "johnism"?

Nicole just txt'd "Happiness is different for everyone" and that is an excellent summary of my current state. If it is "different for everyone" it is ultimately meaningless or scrubbed of meaning by a superfluity of various (and often conflicting) iterations. Is it not? That's what my mind says today. I must say that it literally hurts my head to have my thinking fail so; to become so circular and self-referential (meaningless?). Sometimes I'm just happy for people to talk to because they may well say, "No, you're wrong. Shut-up. That's not it. Idiot! It's not like that!" And today I feel that I mostly agree: This is useless; it's not even progressing.

It's circular and masturbatory and I'm stuck in the middle of it. I can't think anymore except like this. It makes me feel infantile. I just took an interesting break to txt Nicole who thinks this is all merely "word games." I see what she is saying and worry that perhaps she's right, but that I can no longer avoid them. Though I struggle to experience this whole process as a 'playing' or a 'game', but perhaps that is my ultimate problem, to have lost the sense of playing? If I'm playing this, am I having fun? The real rub seems to be that it feels like thinking itself has been rendered useless. This is probably fine if everything is playing. But, if it is, is "knowing" supposed to help? Make it easier? Is there a degree to which "I" want this to be "serious"? Am I simply putting too many quotation marks around life again? Does the degree to which I want this to be serious put the power in the hands of others, such that it IS something only if people agree that it is?

For example, if someone paid me some money to do just this, would that, in turn, make it right? Worthy? Well, the worth would probably be strictly monetary. IF one is to argue for an inherent worth, would it not have to be done gratis? What if someone gave me an obscene amount of money? Probably no effect on non-monetary meaning, but do we live in a society that would view that "value" as the most important and arguably only quantifiable one? Getting paid to do something is tangible and valuable in so far as somewhat necessary, but this takes everything back to Christ's assertion (camel through the eye of needle easier than a rich man entering heaven) and Freedom v. Possession.

What does this mean: money = real | real = life | life = thought | thought = imaginary? If any of the above are true, though, then the monetary is as unreal as anything else? What is real? Nothing? If you argue that nothing is real, can any of it have any meaning? If you want something to have meaning, do you not therefore HAVE to argue that something is real? And, even if money is a representative fiction, does it still not hold the only societally agreed upon representation of value?

A friend just txted me fantasy football questions. That is also just like life. It's an ultimately meaningless collection of players, points, and outcomes that we *create* meaning for through "caring" as reflected by our use of money, love, and time. The brain is a powerful tool to "see" anything you put into it. Does it make it, or just see it? Does it matter? Isn't that what the subjective idealists have been saying all along? Make your world by thinking it into being?

Again, I ask, what is the point of this story? Why am I thinking it? Is it fun or true or both? These are the important questions. Why am I doing this? The answer seems to be to reason out some way – that's a laughable choice of words "reason." To *make* (also laughable)… I want to make my brain correspond to the thought that one creates one's world by thinking it into being. That brings me back, once more, to why this one? Why not? Is that sufficient? I just texted friends and ended one about fantasy football: "LOL & Mocking on Tuesday!" That seems like the perfect subtitle to my story. Shakespeare wrote in *Macbeth* that life is a poor player who struts and frets his hour upon the stage and is heard no more. It is a tale told by an idiot, full of sound and fury, signifying nothing. Wow… calling it meaningless is so much less poetic. IF Macbeth had a Tuesday (and we all know he did not), he would undoubtedly be mocked endlessly. *LoL & Mocking on Tuesday* = life.

If that's true, if the only thing to do is Eat, Drink, and Be Merry for tomorrow you may be in Utah, then one can think like this. If it makes one happy …does it make me happy? Is doing it a way to confront death? Is everything I think a way to confront death? Woody Allen said everything is a way to confront, elude, or evade death – even sex. Freud said everything is directed towards getting sex (or spreading the DNA or genetic code). Either way, between the two of them they have covered everything. Thus, another sub-title could be *Woody & Sigmund*. It has a ring.

What else can be thought... felt? This? This seems to do nothing for me but diminish my chances of either. Well, if it could be 'solved' or 'thought out' maybe it could be described as a way to transcend death, but it's not. This is not "thinking". This, if it is anything, would seem to represent the failure of thinking. Or, at the very least, it represents the failure of my belief in the efficacy of my own thinking.

Now I'm thinking about *Death: or The Playground* or *The Subplot of Subtitles*[17] specifically. God, I love a good subtitle. Maybe I need one for my life. Maybe one of these is that very thing. Maybe it is, to parenthetically warp a famous philosophical maxim, "I think (poorly) therefore I am (poorly)." Does that follow from "I think therefore I am?" - Descartes' single and irreducible fact, upon which he based an entire weltanschauung? His personal Sine Qua Non reduced to my muddy musing through my failure to think properly.

Finally, Nicole had enough of my rambling and said, "Go dig a ditch." This is very good advice. The Buddhists would say, "Chop wood / Carry water." Whatever you say or do about the meaning of life you

---

[17] The Subplot of Subtitles is a particular obsession/expression within *Death: or The Playground*.

chop wood and carry water. So, just keep doing that and leave the Four Noble Truths to Nagarjuna as just that: Unsolvable, Unanswerable, Neither Real nor Not Real. Both and Not Both. Quantum physics tells us this is true in that a "particle" can both go through and not go through a slot. It only does one when it is measured, before that it does both and neither. They say this is scientifically provable. Also, electrons can be located (at least a probability) or the speed can be measured, but not both. Is this merely a limitation of measurement? It is speculated that when electrons are not measured, they are not somewhere as yet unmeasurable, they are simply nowhere specific. This seems exactly like my thinking right now. When Nicole says go dig a ditch to me, I can only think, "If I dig a ditch in a circle, is it still a ditch?" Or, perhaps more to the point, does it "Flow" in any meaningful way? Maybe it's just a moat? If I were to write a poem now it would simply be a circle (though not a perfect circle, perhaps symbolically so). If ever something represented the problem with words, I think it's the perfect circle. The number π is related to the perfect circle, but it never repeats itself. It is 3.14159-ad infinitum and continuing to use the language of mathematics to come up with new arrangements of numbers that would never, ever, ever, repeat? We simply cannot hold that thought in our brains. We can think around, near, or about, but we can't really have the thought. We can use a symbol to reflect what we say it means to us or means mathematically, but it is still only an idea. Math is an idea. It is a language. So is everything. So is this. Does that realization help? I can't see how it can do anything other than prove the uselessness of my own thought (or do I just mean unoriginality?). I can't invent a story wherein my perceived lack of thought is useful, except to say "Keep playing in the playdoh!" The Buddhists said "Chop wood / carry water" years ago. Are we still circling the same question?

If thinking really has failed, then what? My "failed" thoughts have run to A: material vs. mental, and B: All thinking is circular or so vague as to be meaninglessly relative. If this is so, are not experiencing and doing and feeling as well? "Feeling" is an illusion... Ultimately meaning is just ____, and I mean "just" or "whatever" or "chop wood, carry water". There is nothing but relativity and nonsense or "thus"-ness. If one cannot think, feel, experience something concrete and independently meaningful (not merely relativistically so) then what is the point? Unknowable to a finite mind?

Why? Why would any of this be helpful let alone a "realization?" And arguably it is not so. What does that argument look like? My brain does useless things and I'm merely stuck with this uselessness because that is how it is? Is the teleology of the argument "useless" self-defeating (illogical in even a Darwinian sense)? I seem to do many things that I would describe as "useful" from my individualistic perspective, but surely not this.

One may accept the fact we are here (our presence or thinking in a Cartesian sense) as the ultimate Tat Tvam Asi or QED if one likes, but it does not seem to reduce the importance or need to understand even if it robs it of concepts like "ultimate meaning." One simple division that occupies most of mankind is that there seem to be two competing camps. A: Power, stuff, money (one could say atheism or agnosticism or materialism) and B: God / Religion / imagination (Christ, Buddha, Mohammed, Lao Tse, Confuscious, you name it – Dahli Lama or even Mao. Though the latter may have been a staunch "A", I list him in order to demonstrate that religion doesn't have to be part of the thought, only worship or 'faith' or belief.

They also blend. Some people worship sports or acting stars or "fame" or "power" and some people we'd call doers are very religious at the same time. However, there is probably one "more ultimate" truth for them. Some athletes would tithe, but not give up their talent/wealth/fame (sport) for anything, including god. And some are the opposite; though one wonders how many would give the entirety of their wealth to the church when it plainly says in the bible they will receive three times the amount back from god. Apparently they do not believe this enough to affect their actions. Aha –faith as measured by materialism! How contradictory. Some people are forced to give up their sport/talent and find "god" through the process. At any rate, when push comes to shove or when an individual is given an Abrahamesque or Jobesque test, THAT is when they are able to know whether they are more about "mental/spiritual" or "material". It has been one of the most brilliant legacies of Christianity to insist that God's blessing or spiritual blessing or worthiness cannot be measured through physical/worldly success -Job.

On the other hand "god" seems to subsume stories to his/her own story, while many of his/her followers (Buddhist, Christian, Homeless) seem to need to evade (monastery, faith, the world) the A-types to survive. Sometimes faith or belief can be negating to one's own story (i.e. the latter is a "proudness" or superstition and only the one story ("illusion?") is "real". Are A & B really at odds for an ultimate (there's that word again) answer, or is their dichotomy simply set up by the premise (my premise) that things are mostly one or the other (there's the circularity).

Do all questions come down to, "Are we meant to play ***successfully*** in the playdoh?" IS it relative? Could all this "thinking" be reduced to a sort of effort to defend the relative failure of *Death: or The Playground* or *Girl Eleven*[18]? What am "I" trying to "prove" or "discover" (back to square one)?

Me? My existence?

Why am I trying to "prove" that? Is the QED I started with insufficient? Is the phrase "QED I started with" rhetorical, senseless, cart-before-the-horse, meaningless? Are Rene and the Cartesian world-view holders immune to the discussion vis-à-vis their ur-stance? Meaning, if I "think" what I really want is for things to make sense. I want their meaning to be... to be... what? I want thinking to be effective, or at least have the potential to be, and not mere "thusness" or ontic or this seemingly circular, endless, inescapable parade.

---

[18] *Girl Eleven* is a script written by John Cady in 2010.

If "playing in the playdoh" is the most dissatisfying story one might come up with (meaningless), then any God or Xenu in providing "meaning" (regardless of their verisimilitude) are superior. Because that's "ultimately" what johnism does, it flies in the face of "what is" so much (as it is) because it merely mocks religion (all religion). It glorifies beliefs and places absolutely relative and circular judgments on everything that purports to be not so (including, especially including, meaning).

This brings us to one of my favorite topics: Mockery. What is the meaning of mockery? Is it the ultimate Pooh, Clouseau, Quixote, Catch-22 of life? Is Ignatius J. Reilly right or bad or are those the wrong questions? Doomed? Surely. What does it mean? (AGAIN). We laugh therefore we are? Find the humor, find the joy in this sad accident? Is that it? Is that what mockery is – an ultimate *not taking seriously*? But then who or what is not being taken seriously? Other gods? Other belief systems? The prophet Mohammed? Is that the appeal of mockery, everything from Christ and the Buddha to atheism, agnosticism and Chairman Mao is not taken seriously? It is threatened and treated as an inferior to the superior "mockery" in one swell foop (as Clouseau would have it)?

There is seriousness to that! Is god the joke that is so funny it transcends (or creates) mockery. Monty Python produced a sketch about a "Joke that was so funny you die laughing." At the time of my discovery, I enjoyed wondering if that was God: *The Joke that's so funny you die laughing*. Now that is irony and mockery and... probably bad thinking. But, if everything comes down to mockery, then worshipping it is not a bad idea regardless of the outcome. It's all that is.

But how? How does one seriously worship something that requires the seriousness to be made fun of and "mocked." Is that a self-fulfilling, tautological, nonsensical circle? Is that what I started with? Is this *johnism*? It seems boring, though, because it is rooted in "reality" or time / space / direction and therefore not as pleasing to finite beings as things which purport not to be finite, even if they cannot be thought. This seems to advocate mockery while you're alive and boredom when you're dead (because it's no longer funny?). Anything not rooted in time / space / direction is impossible to take seriously and therefore cannot be mocked. Is the real trick knowing when to stop? Stop when you run into the back of your previous thought.

Epilogue

...turns out it's ALL real and none of it true.

Afterword by Dr. Dave Jamison

(An Apology)

John Cady's *eXistEntiAlasM* seems to me to be something John Kennedy Toole's Ignatius J. Reilly would have written if he were as talented as Dave Eggers.[19] That claim might have something to do with the title of Cady's first chapter, "A Heartrending Work of Stupefying Brilliance," an ode to Eggers' novel *A Heartbreaking Work of Staggering Genius*. To really get John's irreverence, it would be a good idea to take a crack at that novel. I remember in my early 20s being stupefied at having enough confidence in your writing to call your book *A Heartbreaking Work of Staggering Genius*, and then to actually turn around and pull it off. People were so flummoxed by the title that they did not want to like the book, but it only takes about twenty pages to realize that it is the perfect title, for two reasons:

First, Eggers' book is written with a casual expertise that makes reading his prose feel like you are with a

---

[19] Toole wrote *A Confederacy of Dunces*

friend on their yacht and they are pouring you champagne. He washes you over with words, and soon everything is alright and you are going to be taken care of for the entire book. It is a decadent literary experience. And the topic *is* heartbreaking, the deaths of his parents. The title is not an exaggeration; not bitingly ironic. It is actually simply a good title for what that book is.

But Second, the title is a defiantly self-assured artistic statement. It is this:

> *This book is a work of genius. There are book critics out there who might disagree with me, but they are wrong. Even though I know it is their job to tell you how good my book is, I am here to say that I do not recognize Book Critics' authority to determine whether this is an expertly written and pure expression of my unconscious soul, because I know that it is. I know it is, like religion. I know it is because this time, this once, as an artist, I managed to open up the vein of the Godhead of True Art, and while writing this work I managed to keep it open till the last page. This book isn't genius because I am such a good writer, it is because I am a good enough writer to know when a writer, when any writer, writes a manifestly inspired work, even if it's me. I am a good*

enough writer to assess any critic out there. Therefore, the title of my book is also my review.

Like Dave Eggers, John Cady is not a writer. He is an artist. Writing is his form, or the form he is taking today (Today, for you. He took the form to write this book long ago and has since shed it), but he could take any artistic form and express his art through it. As such, John is not interested in writing conventions. That is not to say he does not know them. He is highly trained. But he is confident enough in his writing to know why he is rejecting this or that convention, and then to make up a new one, on the spot, that better jibes with the artistic statement he is making at the moment. That is how his mind works. Have you ever seen Laurie Anderson? You get very soon after she starts interacting with you (not that I have, it's just what I imagine. I'm right, though) that she is not particularly interested in doing anything other than figuring out how you in this moment fit into her larger art piece called Life. Warhol was like that, too (No, I did not know Warhol.) When people like this wake up in the morning, all they do is begin to process how the input they are experiencing works into their Life piece. Some of them, like Warhol and Anderson, actually get jobs as artists, but that is only convenient. Because otherwise they would have simply been that Weird Person Who Works at the Video Store Who's Always Talking About "Society."

They don't have video stores anymore.

Artists are working; John is ever working. This book is a piece; the struggle he put in to publish it was a piece because he will probably write about it; his pieces are pieces because he writes essays like they are movements in an as-yet-unseen poetry cycle; your reaction to this book will be a piece because he will craft a story around it and tell it at a party while making the listeners martinis.

You think I am joking, but I am not.

The critiques:
There is the occasional drifting into the world of the internal monologue. The world where conversations and movies John saw are always replaying, and he grabs snippets of them and sticks them into his prose as if the rest of the world is hearing the voices. I know how that sounds and I mean it. To really get John's irreverence, you cannot expect that you are supposed to literally connect every reference. *You are supposed to connect to the craft of referencing.* You are supposed to let Bacchus pour you some wine, and entertain revelers with Him at your table . . . not to

any particular end or resolution, but simply to be there reveling for awhile.

John's words are revelry, his writings washing over you like a warm river;
writhing, warm rivulets resting,
then wresting,
then resting.

Don't try to read his essays too hard, or find the underlying veneer of caustic self-hate. It isn't there. John is not here to remind you of how your not-lived-up-to life is really your mom or stepdad's fault. The insecure whining disguised as "ascerbic wit" in American culture is thoroughly dismembered by John's constantly reminding us of the fact that most human conflict is ultimately, endlessly mercilessly absurd considering this soft warm planet that we have settled into and made our own. We have so thoroughly decimated and cowed every other living organism on Earth with such ruthless mastery that the fact that all we end up doing then is just turning on each other is just too hilarious to fret over. Like, are you freaking *kidding* me? Have some wine!

Seriously. I suggest it now. With a friend. John would want you to. And I want you two to, too.

David Jamison
Jacksonville, FL 2021
www.davidmichaeljamison.com

About the Author

John Cady is a writer, director, producer, actor, and CEO living in Denver, CO. He has co-authored another book *So You Want To Be In Show Business* with his agent Steve Stevens.

He also co-authored *Death: or The Playground*, a play originally produced in Los Angeles at the Stella Adler Theatre. He shares creative control for KDworld.net with his brother.